大地英豪

The Last of the Mohicans

最後一個摩希根人

原著∗James Fenimore Cooper
改寫∗Janet Olearski
譯者∗安卡斯

ABOUT THIS BOOK

For the Student

 Listen to the story and do some activities on your Audio CD.

 Talk about the story.

For the Teacher

Go to our Readers Resource site for information on using readers and downloadable Resource Sheets, photocopiable Worksheets, and Tapescripts. www.helblingreaders.com

For lots of great ideas on using Graded Readers consult Reading Matters, the Teacher's Guide to using Helbling Readers.

Structures

Sequencing of future tenses	• Could / was able to / managed to
Present perfect plus yet, already, just	• Had to / didn't have to
First conditional	• Shall / could for offers
Present and past passive	• May / can / could for permission • Might for future possibility
How long?	• Make and let
Very / really / quite	• Causative have • Want / ask / tell someone to do something

Structures from lower levels are also included.

CONTENTS

ABOUT THE AUTHOR

James Fenimore Cooper was born in Burlington, New Jersey, USA in 1789. He was the eleventh of twelve children. His parents, William and Elizabeth Fenimore Cooper, were Quakers[1]. His father was a successful landowner[2] and he established the village of Cooperstown in New York State. When Cooper was growing up, he loved exploring the countryside and forests that surrounded his family's estate[3].

Cooper joined the Navy when he was 17 and traveled the seas for the next five years. He inherited[4] his father's estate when he was 20, and got married when he was 22. For a while he made a living from farming. He lived comfortably and had time for activities such as reading. He learned about American history and about the lives of the Native Americans.

Once, after finishing a story he told his wife that he could easily write something better himself. She told him to try. He did, and published his first novel in 1820. He went on[5] to write over 40 books, including works of social and political criticism.

He is most famous for his five 'Leatherstocking Tales' set in the American frontier[6] which include *The Last of the Mohicans* (1826). The hero of these novels is Natty Bumppo, who is also known as Hawkeye and as Leatherstocking.

From 1826 to 1833 Cooper traveled in Europe and lived in London, Paris and Sorrento. Through his writing he aimed[7] to teach his readers about social responsibilities, about democracy and about American history and heritage[8].

Cooper died in 1851 at his home in Cooperstown.

---

1 Quaker [ˈkwekɚ] (n.) 貴格會教徒
2 landowner [ˈlændˌlɔrd] (n.) 地主
3 estate [ɪsˈtet] (n.) 地產
4 inherit [ɪnˈhɛrɪt] (v.) 繼承
5 go on 繼續下去
6 American frontier 美國初期的殖民拓荒者
7 aim [em] (v.) 致力；旨在
8 heritage [ˈhɛrətɪdʒ] (n.) 遺產

The Last of the Mohicans is set in the summer of 1757. This was the time of the French and Indian War, when the British and the French armies were both trying to gain[1] control of an area of West New York State.

Fort William Henry, a British outpost controlled by Colonel Munro, is under attack by the French General Montcalm and his Indian allies[2], amongst them the Huron and the Delaware tribes. Munro's daughters, Alice and Cora, are on their way to join their father. They are captured by Magua, a Huron Indian who wants revenge[3] on his old enemy Munro.

The sisters are helped by an expert frontiersman[4] called Hawkeye, and his Mohican companions Chingachgook and Uncas. After a series of terrible battles[5] and thrilling[6] escapes, the story has a tragic, though positive, ending.

The Last of the Mohicans is a work of fiction, but some parts of the story, such as the surrender[7] of Fort William Henry in August 1757, are based on real events from history. The colonists left the fort after surrendering, but they were attacked by the Indian allies of the French, and around 180 of them were killed.

---

1 gain [gen] (v.) 贏得
2 ally [ˈælaɪ] (n.) 同盟者
3 revenge [rɪˈvɛndʒ] (n.) 報仇
4 frontiersman [frʌnˈtɪrzmən] (n.) 拓荒者
5 battle [ˈbætl̩] (n.) 戰役
6 thrilling [ˈθrɪlɪŋ] (a.) 令人顫慄的
7 surrender [səˈrɛndɚ] (n.) 投降

1 Look at these pictures of three characters from the book. Who do you think they are? Where are they from? What are they like? Write five words or phrases to describe their character.

Chingachgook

Hawkeye

Magua

2 If you were going on a long journey, which of the men above would you choose to be your guide? Discuss your reasons with your partner.

3 Imagine you are travelling through the woods with your guide. Hostile Indians are trying to find you. Read the list below. Put a tick (✓) next to the things you should do and a cross (×) next to things you should not do.

_____ 1 Use your rifle to kill animals for food.
_____ 2 Sing, so you won't be bored on the trip.
_____ 3 Use a bow and arrow.
_____ 4 Hide your horses.
_____ 5 Wear your walking boots.
_____ 6 Leave behind any clothes you don't need.
_____ 7 Take turns with your companions to keep watch at night.
_____ 8 Leave the food you don't eat for the wolves.
_____ 9 Make sure you walk on the grass, not on wood or stones.

4 Match the words from the story with the pictures.

_____ a) tomahawk   _____ e) canoe
_____ b) wigwam   _____ f) rifle
_____ c) moccasins   _____ g) knife
_____ d) cave   _____ h) hoofs

5 Now use each of the words above to complete the sentences.

1. They came across the water in a large _____.
2. Suddenly they heard the sound of horses' _____.
3. It's easier to walk in _____ than in boots.
4. A tall, powerful Huron ran towards him, waving his _____ in the air.
5. Hawkeye grabbed the _____ and stabbed it through the Indian's heart.
6. The _____ of Magua is empty. He needs a wife and children of his own.
7. He saw the bear sitting in a dark corner of the _____
8. Hawkeye aimed his _____ and fired.

6 Choose one of the sentences above. Write what happens next.

7 Read these sentences from the story. They describe sounds made by objects or animals. Listen and match the underlined words with the sound you hear.

_____ a Suddenly they heard the sttound of <u>horses' hoofs</u>.
_____ b Before Uncas could move, the wolves <u>howled</u> and ran away into the forest.
_____ c The bear <u>growled</u> at Heyward.
_____ d Bullets <u>whizzed</u> over the men's heads.
_____ e If there is a problem, <u>croak</u> three times like a crow.
_____ f He heard the <u>crack</u> of a rifle.

8 Listen to the opening of the story. Tick (✓) if you think the following sentences are True (T) or False (F). Discuss the reasons for your answers with a partner.

T F ① Magua wants the people at Fort Edward to feel safe.
T F ② The French commander Montcalm is a cruel man who will torture and kill the soldiers at Fort William Henry.
T F ③ General Webb is a wise and calm man.

9 If you were General Webb, what would you do? Discuss your answer with your partner.

① Send all your soldiers to Fort William Henry.
② Send no soldiers to Fort William Henry.
③ Leave Fort Edward and move to a safer place.
④ Do something else. (Decide with your partner what you would do.)

🗣 **10** Look at this scene from *The Last of the Mohicans.*
In pairs decide a title for it.

🗣 **11** Look at the picture above for 2 minutes then test each
other. Ask questions such as:

- How many people are in the picture?
- Who are the main characters in the picture?
- Who is in the background?
- What is happening?

12 The story is set in the American frontier. The frontier was
the division between the settled land where the colonialists
lived in the east, and the unsettled land where the Indians
had their land in the west.

What do you think life was like? Imagine you are a
colonialist. You are moving west to find land and build a
home. Write a letter describing your feelings and what
you bring with you. Describe the journey and what you
hope to find.

CHAPTER 1

Magua traveled for two hours from Fort William Henry. The Indian brave[1] ran most of the way, through thick forests and along hidden paths, to reach Fort Edward. He had important news from Colonel Munro for General Webb, Fort Edward's British commander.

'The French commander Montcalm is coming', said Magua. 'He is marching[2] now towards Fort William Henry.'

Magua's words brought fear to the people who lived inside Fort Edward and to the British soldiers who were camped outside the fort.

'Montcalm is a very great chief[3], said the Indian. 'He has many soldiers and many Indian braves. If Montcalm attacks Fort William Henry, everyone will die. Colonel Munro will die. Montcalm's braves will take many scalps[4] from the British soldiers. Colonel Munro needs more men and supplies[5].'

The inhabitants of Fort Edward were terrified.

General Webb listened quietly to Magua's story. It was true that the war between the French and the British was savage[6] and bloody. The two sides had fought each other for three years to win this wild and hostile country.

---

1 brave [brev] (n.) 在這裡指美國的印地安人戰士
2 march [mɑrtʃ] (v.) 行進；前進行軍
3 chief [tʃif] (n.) 領袖
4 scalp [skælp] (n.) 印第安人從已死敵人頭上剝下來當戰利品的帶髮頭皮
5 supplies [sə`plaɪs] (n.)（作複數形）補給品；軍糧
6 savage [`sævɪdʒ] (a.) 殘酷的；猛烈的

'How many men has Montcalm got?' asked General Webb.

'His soldiers are as numerous as the leaves on the trees,' said Magua. 'You must send many men.'

General Webb was calm.

'You are a brave man,' he said, 'Thank you for this message. I will call you when I need you.'

The following morning fifteen hundred of General Webb's men set off[1] on the journey to Fort William Henry. Ahead of them was a march of one day.

JOURNEYS

★ What is the longest journey you have been on?
★ How did you travel? By car? By plane? By bus?
★ What preparations did you make before the journey?

Outside General Webb's house, servants prepared some horses for a journey. People were curious and came to watch. Among them was David Gamut, a tall thin man with narrow shoulders and long arms.

'These are not ordinary horses,' said Gamut. 'They belong to important people, probably two ladies and an army officer.' The people in the crowd were very impressed[2].

'I'm a preacher but I also buy and sell horses, so I know about these things', explained Gamut. He turned to look at his listeners, but instead he found himself looking into the wild and frightening face of Magua the Indian. Magua was still covered in his warpaint[3], and was armed with a tomahawk[4] and a knife. The two men stared at each other.

At that moment a young army officer and two women came out of the house. Both women wore hats with veils[5] that protected their faces. As the officer helped the younger woman onto her horse, the wind blew her veil aside.

Gamut saw that she had bright blue eyes and long golden hair. The other woman was also beautiful. She was dark-haired and was probably four or five years older. The three riders said goodbye to General Webb and left the camp followed by their servants.

Magua ran behind them. He passed the younger woman's horse, and ran onto the path in front of the riders. The older woman looked at the Indian with a mixture of admiration and pity. The younger woman cried out in alarm[6] when the Indian ran past her horse.

'Don't worry, Alice', said the officer. 'The Indian is an army runner. His name is Magua. He's going to guide us to the lake so that we will reach Fort William Henry before the soldiers.'

'Do you trust[7] him, Heyward?' asked Alice.

'I do', said the officer. 'He used to fight with the Mohawks and once he was an enemy of your father, Colonel Munro, but that was a long time ago. Now he is our friend.'

1 set off 動身出發
2 were impressed 感到佩服
3 warpaint [ˈwɔrˌpent] (n.) 部落戰士在出征前塗在臉上和身上的顏料
4 tomahawk [ˈtɑməˌhɔk] (n.) 北美印第安人的戰斧
5 veil [vel] (n.) 面紗；面罩
6 in alarm 在驚嚇中
7 trust [trʌst] (v.) 信任

🎧 'Does Magua speak English?' said Alice. 'Can you ask him to say something?'

Heyward laughed. 'He pretends he doesn't know any English. He only speaks it if he has to.'

Just then the Indian stopped and pointed to a dark path through the bushes. There was only space for one horse to pass.

'Maybe we should travel with the soldiers,' said Alice. 'I don't feel safe with Magua.'

'Just because he has different manners from us and his skin is dark, it doesn't mean we should distrust him', said the dark-haired woman.

Alice did not reply to her sister. She rode her horse through the bushes and followed Magua down the dark path between the trees.

PREJUDICE

★ Alice does not trust Magua. Is she judging him unfairly?
★ How do you judge people when you meet them for the first time? By the clothes they wear? By the way they speak? By the way they behave? By the color of their skin?

The riders continued through the forest.

'The servants must leave us now and change direction', said Magua. 'Then it will be more difficult for Montcalm's Indians to follow our tracks[1].'

Heyward told the servants to ride in the direction of the soldiers. Then he and the two sisters rode on. Magua ran in front of them. Suddenly they heard the sound of horses' hoofs. The riders held their breath and waited in the bushes to see who was following them. A tall thin man in a blue coat rode into view.

8

'Who are you?' asked Heyward.

'My name is David Gamut. I am a preacher[2] and I sing hymns[3]', said the man.

Alice was delighted[4] when she heard this.

'Please let him travel with us, Heyward', she said. 'I saw him at Fort Edward. Mr Gamut can ride next to me and we will sing together.'

Gamut started singing. But Magua asked Heyward to stop Gamut immediately.

'I'm sorry', said Heyward, 'you have a wonderful singing voice, Mr Gamut, but on this occasion I must ask you to travel in silence.'

'Heyward, why do you have to spoil[5] everything? We were enjoying ourselves', said Alice.

'There will be plenty of opportunities for singing when we arrive at our destination', said Heyward. 'No one knows we are here. Let's make sure it stays that way.'

The four riders passed through the woods, but they did not see the painted face of an Indian watching them from the bushes.

1 tracks [træks] (n.)（作複數形）足跡
2 preacher [ˋpritʃɚ] (n.) 傳教士；牧師
3 hymn [hɪm] (n.) 讚美詩；聖歌
4 delighted [dɪˋlaɪtɪd] (a.) 愉快的；滿意的
5 spoil [spɔɪl] (v.) 破壞

CHAPTER 2

On that July evening, on the banks of a small stream[1], an Indian and a white man rested and talked quietly. The air was silent except for the sound of birdsong and the distant roar of a waterfall. The Indian carried a tomahawk and a knife, and wore no ornaments except for an eagle's feather. He had just one short tuft[2] of hair on his shaven[3] head. Lying across his knees was a rifle[4]. He was not a young man but he looked strong and energetic.

The white man was muscular[5] and suntanned[6] and had an honest face. He wore a green shirt with a yellow fringe, and on his head he had a cap made of animal skins. He wore Indian moccasins and buckskin[7] trousers. In his belt he carried a knife, a pouch[8] and a horn. His long hunting rifle was propped up[9] against a tree. He spoke the language of the Indians and, as he talked, he looked around him as if checking for a hidden enemy.

'We are different, Hawkeye', said the Indian. 'Your fathers came from the setting sun. My fathers came from the red sky of the morning.'

'We came from far away where buffaloes live on the plains[10]', said Chingachgook. 'We reached the big river. There we fought the Alligewi until the ground was red with their blood. We traveled to the salt lake, and the Maquas followed us. We chased them into the woods. Much later the first white men came. They came across the water in a large canoe. We had buried[11] our weapons then, we were one people and we were very happy. We had fish from the lake, deer from the woods, and birds from the air.'

1 stream [strim] (n.) 小河；溪流
2 tuft [tʌft] (n.) (頭髮、羽毛、草等) 一簇；一束
3 shaven [ˋʃevn̩] (a.) 剃光頭的
4 rifle [ˋraɪf!] (n.) 步槍；來福槍
5 muscular [ˋmʌskjələ] (a.) 肌肉發達的；健壯的
6 suntanned [ˋsʌntænd] (a.) 皮膚曬成紅褐色的
7 buckskin [ˋbʌkˏskɪn] (n.) 鹿皮革
8 pouch [paʊtʃ] (n.) 小袋子；煙草袋
9 prop up 支撐起某物
10 plain [plen] (n.) 平原；曠野
11 bury [ˋbɛrɪ] (v.) 埋起來

'I am sure that your fathers were wise men and brave warriors', said Hawkeye.

'It is true that I have the blood of chiefs in my veins[1]', said Chingachgook, 'and my tribe[2] is the grandfather of nations. When the white men came, they gave my people the fire-water[3]. They drank until they thought they had found the Great Spirit. Then they gave away their land little by little, until we lived only in the forests and no longer on the shores[4] of the lake. You know, Hawkeye, I have never visited the graves[5] of my fathers.'

'That's sad', said Hawkeye. 'As for me, I'm sure I won't have a grave. My bones will be left for the wolves. But where are your people now?'

'Where are the flowers of those summers?' said Chingachgook. 'Like the flowers, they all died. Every member of my family has gone now to the land of spirits. Soon it will be my turn and, when Uncas follows in my footsteps[6], there will be no one. My son Uncas is the last of the Mohicans.'

'Who is talking about me?' said a voice.

1 vein [ven] (n.) 血管
2 tribe [traɪb] (n.) 部落
3 fire-water [ˈfaɪrˌwɔtɚ] (n.) 酒
4 shore [ʃor] (n.) （海、湖或河的）岸；濱
5 grave [grev] (n.) 墓穴；埋葬處
6 follow in my footsteps 跟隨我的腳步；步上我的後塵
7 coward [ˈkauəd] (n.) 懦夫
8 crawl [krɔl] (v.) 爬行；緩慢地移動
9 arrow [ˈæro] (n.) 箭
10 bow [bo] (n.) 弓

A young warrior joined them and sat down on the bank. Chingachgook looked at his son and asked, 'So, have you seen any Hurons in these woods?'

'There must be ten of them, but they are hiding like cowards[7]', said Uncas.

'They want scalps and money', said Hawkeye. 'They are working for Montcalm.'

'Then, we will chase them out of the bushes like deer', said Uncas.

'I have a better idea', said Hawkeye, 'Let's eat tonight and then go hunting for the Hurons tomorrow.' Hawkeye looked around him. 'There's our dinner', he said pointing to a deer in the distance.

Uncas crawled[8] into the bushes. He put an arrow[9] in his bow[10], took aim and shot the deer.

'Listen', whispered Hawkeye, 'more deer are coming.'

Chingachgook put his ear to the ground and listened. 'No', he said, 'White men are coming on their horses.'

CHAPTER 3

 Heyward saw a man on the path in front of him. A rifle was resting on the man's arm and his finger was on the trigger[1].

'Who is there?' said Hawkeye.

'Followers of God, the law[2] and the king', said Heyward. 'We've been travelling through this forest since sunrise. We're tired and we haven't eaten. Are we far from Fort William Henry?'

'You're lost', said Hawkeye. 'You should follow the river to Fort Edward.'

'But we left Fort Edward this morning', said Heyward. 'Our Indian guide led us here, but now we don't know where we are.'

'Indians find their way using the deer paths, the stars and the streams', said Hawkeye. 'It's impossible for them to get lost. What tribe is your Indian from?'

'He's a Huron', said Heyward.

Chingachgook and Uncas jumped to their feet.

'A Huron!' said Hawkeye. 'The Hurons are thieves[3]. You're lucky that only one of them is with you.'

'Our guide was brought up[4] by the Mohawks. His name is Magua. He is our friend. Now please answer my question. How far are we from Fort William Henry?'

'How do I know that you're not a spy[5]?' said Hawkeye.

'I'm an officer from Fort William Henry', said Heyward. 'I'm escorting[6] Colonel Munro's daughters, Alice and Cora, to join their father. We took a short path, guided by our Indian scout[7].'

'And he deceived[8] you and deserted[9]', said Hawkeye.

'No, he didn't. He's here with us, at the back of the group', said Heyward.

'Well, then I'd like to take a look at him', said Hawkeye.

Hawkeye entered the bushes and after just a few steps he met the two women and the preacher who were waiting anxiously[10] on their horses. Behind them, Magua was leaning[11] against a tree. Hawkeye studied him carefully. He did not move, but he had a dark look on his face. Hawkeye returned to Heyward.

'He's a Huron', whispered Hawkeye. 'No Mohawks or any other tribes can change him. I wouldn't stay in these woods at night with that Indian. I could take you back to Fort Edward myself in just an hour, but with the women in your company, that's impossible. These woods are full of Montcalm's braves and your Indian Magua knows where to find them. He intended to lead you to the French. Colonel Munro's daughters would be an excellent prize.' Hawkeye looked back through the trees to where Magua was standing. He lifted his rifle and took aim[12].

---

1 trigger ['trɪgɚ] (n.) 扳機
2 law [lɔ] (n.) 律法
3 thief [θif] (n.) 小偷；賊
4 bring up 養育
5 spy [spaɪ] (n.) 間諜
6 escort [ɪ'skɔrt] (v.) 護送

7 scout [skaʊt] (n.) 偵察兵
8 deceive [dɪ'siv] (v.) 欺騙
9 desert [dɪ'zɝt] (v.) 遺棄
10 anxiously ['æŋkʃəslɪ] (adv.) 焦急地
11 lean [lin] (v.) 倚；靠
12 take aim 瞄準

 'No', said Heyward, 'Don't shoot.'

'Very well', said Hawkeye. He spoke quietly to Chingachgook and Uncas in their language, then they both disappeared into the woods.

'Go and speak to Magua', said Hawkeye to Heyward. 'Try to distract[1] him.'

Heyward trotted[2] his horse through the bushes to the place where Magua was resting.

'It seems we are a long way from the fort', said Heyward. Magua stared at him. 'The scout will help us find our way.'

'So, you do not need me', said Magua. 'I will travel to the fort alone.'

'Stay and eat', said Heyward, 'then we will travel to the fort in the morning. We're all tired. Let us rest so that we are fresh for our journey tomorrow.'

---

1 distract [dɪˋstrækt] (v.) 使分心；引開
2 trot [trɑt] (v.) 騎馬小跑
3 mumble [ˋmʌmbl̩] (v.) 含糊地說
4 rustle [ˋrʌsl̩] (v.)（綢衣、樹葉、紙等）沙沙作響

Magua mumbled[3] something to himself, then he took a small pouch of dried meat from his belt. He started to eat the food, but all the time he looked around him to the left and to the right.

Suddenly some leaves rustled[4]. Magua turned his ear towards the sound. At that moment Uncas and his father, covered in their warpaint, stepped out of the bushes. But Magua was already on his feet and, as fast as the wind, he ran away through the forest. There was a sudden flash of light as Hawkeye fired his rifle.

TRUST

* Neither Hawkeye nor Alice trust Magua. Why?
* Have you ever been in a situation where you distrusted someone?

CHAPTER 4

 Hawkeye, Uncas and Chingachgook returned from the forest without Magua.

'He was too fast for us', said Hawkeye, 'but I think I wounded[1] him.'

'If he's wounded, he won't go very far', said Heyward. 'Let's follow him. We can easily catch him.'

'If we follow him, my friend, he will lead us straight into an ambush[2]', said Hawkeye. 'Do you want our scalps to be hanging outside Montcalm's tent tomorrow?'

Heyward was horrified[3] at this thought. 'Guide us to the fort', he said. 'I'll pay you.'

'We want no payment', said Hawkeye, 'but all of you must be completely silent during our journey. We will take you to a secret place and we will hide the horses so that Magua's men cannot follow our tracks.'

On the river bank the Indians took out a canoe that was hidden in the bushes. Cora, Alice and Gamut climbed in, and Hawkeye and Heyward guided the canoe through the water. Soon they could hear the sound of a waterfall. Heyward climbed into the front of the canoe. Hawkeye sat in the back and used a pole[4] to push the canoe away from the rocks and into the fast current[5] of the river.

The power of the water rocked[6] them in all directions. The canoe's passengers were too terrified to move. Suddenly the canoe plunged[7] through the water out of control. Alice covered her face in terror. Then the canoe stopped its movement. It floated[8] by the side of a rock.

'Climb onto the rocks quickly and wait for me', said Hawkeye.

The passengers climbed safely onto the rock and waited nervously in the dark, afraid to move, and afraid of falling into the black water below them.

A few minutes passed and Hawkeye reappeared with Chingachgook and Uncas, and the carcass[9] of a young deer.

'Did you see any Indians?' asked Heyward.

'We saw wolves', said Hawkeye. 'This means the Indians are following us. The wolves eat the food the Indians leave.'

The two Indians followed Hawkeye along the edge of the rocks and then all three disappeared into the front of the rock. In the darkness, Heyward and his companions could hear voices. There was a sudden blaze[10] of light, and Heyward could see that in the rock there was a deep cavern[11]. A heavy blanket hid its entrance. Hawkeye was holding a burning torch[12].

'Hurry up and come in', said Hawkeye. 'We don't want the Hurons to see the light.'

Inside Hawkeye cooked the meat over a fire. 'Make yourselves comfortable', he said. 'The food is simple, but good.'

'Will we be safe here?' asked Heyward.

Chingachgook lifted another blanket at the back of the cave. It hid the entrance to another cave just like the first one.

Hawkeye laughed. 'We are like old foxes. You won't find us in a burrow[13] with just one hole. We are safe here. The waterfalls are on two sides of us and the river surrounds[14] us.'

---

1 wound [wund] (v.) 使受傷
2 ambush ['æmbuʃ] (n.) 埋伏
3 horrified ['hɔrə,faɪd] (a.) 害怕的
4 pole [pol] (n.) 竿子；柱子
5 current ['kɜ·ənt] (n.) 水流
6 rocked [rɑk] (v.) 使搖擺
7 plunge [plʌndʒ] (v.) (船隻)顛簸
8 float [flot] (v.) 漂浮
9 carcass ['kɑrkəs] (n.) 動物的屍體
10 blaze [blez] (n.) 火焰
11 cavern ['kævən] (n.) 洞穴；山洞
12 torch [tɔrtʃ] (n.) 火炬
13 burrow ['bɝo] (n.) (兔、狐等的) 洞穴；地道
14 surround [sə'raund] (v.) 包圍

Uncas served them with the meat. When he passed the food to Cora, he paused to watch her. Once or twice he spoke in English, attracting the admiration of both sisters. Hawkeye ate his meal, pausing now and then to listen for distant[1] or unusual sounds.

'What's your name?' he asked the preacher.

'Gamut – David Gamut.'

'A very good name', said Hawkeye. 'The Indians have very special names. Chingachgook means Big Snake. That doesn't mean that he is like a snake but that he is silent and attacks his enemies when they don't expect it. So, what exactly is your job, Mr Gamut?' asked Hawkeye.

NAMES

★ People's names often have special meanings. What about your name? Do you know what it means?
★ What is the origin of your name?
★ Does anyone else in your family have the same name?
★ If you had an Indian name, what would it be?

'I'm a preacher.'

'Can you use a rifle?'

'No, I thank God that I never needed to learn. I just teach the singing of hymns.'

'That's strange work', said Hawkeye. 'Well, why don't you sing us a hymn before we go to sleep?'

'With great pleasure', said Gamut. When the preacher sang, Alice and Cora joined in. Halfway through their song a terrible cry filled the air.

'Perhaps the Indians can see the light of our fire', said Heyward.

'No', said Hawkeye, 'they can't see our hiding place. There is no danger. Now get some rest. We'll leave tomorrow before sunrise.'

1 distant [ˋdɪstənt] (a.) 遠的

CHAPTER 5

 During the night they heard the cry again. Hawkeye and the Mohicans went outside to stand guard. Heyward joined them. The air outside the cave was cool. The same cry came from the direction of the river.

'It's the horses', said Heyward. 'The wolves are close and the horses can smell them.'

'Go and throw a lighted torch into the pack of wolves', Hawkeye told Uncas. 'Otherwise we'll have no horses in the morning.' Before Uncas could move, the wolves howled[1] and ran away into the forest.

'We must hide', said Hawkeye. 'Stay silent and wait.'

As the hours passed, Cora and Alice fell asleep in each other's arms. Heyward sat against the rocks and dozed[2]. Gamut lay fast asleep. Only Hawkeye and the Mohicans stayed awake. They watched the trees and the shore. They listened for every tiny[3] sound.

Before dawn[4] Hawkeye woke Heyward.

'It's time to leave', he said. 'Be ready to get into the canoe when I bring it to the landing-place[5].'

'I'm sorry. I fell asleep', said Heyward. 'Is everything all right?'

'All is well', said Hawkeye, and he disappeared into the darkness to get the canoe.

'Cora! Alice! Wake up', said Heyward.

But just at that moment the air filled with terrifying screams and cries. The women shrieked[6] in terror. Gamut stood up.

'What's happening?', he shouted.

'The Indians', shouted Heyward. 'Get down!'

They saw flashes of gunfire coming from the river bank. There was a sudden crack[7] of rifle fire nearby. Gamut fell down onto the rocks. The Indians on the bank shouted triumphantly[8] when they saw Gamut fall. The Mohicans fired back. There was no sign of Hawkeye. Heyward listened anxiously for the return of the canoe. There was a scream from the river below. Hawkeye's rifle had hit someone. The Indians ran away and everything was silent.

1 howl [haʊl] (v.) 嗥叫；怒吼
2 doze [doz] (v.) 打瞌睡；打盹
3 tiny [ˋtaɪnɪ] (a.) 極小的
4 dawn [dɔn] (n.) 黎明
5 landing-place [ˋlændɪŋˋples] (n.) 上岸處
6 shriek [ʃrik] (v.) 尖叫
7 crack [kræk] (n.) 爆裂聲
8 triumphantly [traɪˋʌmfəntlɪ] (adv.) 勝利地

Heyward pulled Gamut to the safety of the rocks.

'He's alive', said Hawkeye. 'It's just a graze[1]. He's lucky. He'll be more careful next time.'

'Will the Indians come back?' said Heyward.

'They will', said Hawkeye, 'as soon as they have a new plan of attack.'

The men kept watch[2] for a long time, but there was no sign of the Indians.

'I don't think they are coming back', said Heyward.

'You don't know the Hurons. They want our scalps', said Hawkeye. 'Now they know how many of us there are and what weapons[3] we have. They'll come back.'

As he spoke Hawkeye saw some Indians hidden in the nearby rocks. At that moment the woods were filled with more war cries. Four Indians ran across the rocks yelling and screaming. Hawkeye and Uncas aimed their rifles and fired. Two Indians fell to the ground.

Hawkeye and Heyward rushed down the rocks, shooting their guns at the same time. A huge Indian ran towards Hawkeye with a knife. Hawkeye and the Indian struggled. Hawkeye grabbed[4] the knife and stabbed it through the Indian's heart.

Another Indian attacked Heyward. The two men rolled to the edge of the rocks. The Indian grabbed Heyward's neck and squeezed[5] his throat tightly. The Indian tried to strangle[6] Heyward. Suddenly Heyward saw the flash of a knife. Uncas was holding the knife. Blood dripped[7] from its blade[8]. The Indian fell backwards down the rocks. Blood was running from his wrist.

---

1 graze [grez] (n.) 擦傷
2 keep watch 留意
3 weapon ['wɛpən] (n.) 武器
4 grab [græb] (v.) 抓住
5 squeeze [skwiz] (v.) 壓；擠
6 strangle ['stræŋgl] (v.) 扼住；使窒息
7 drip [drɪp] (v.) 滴下
8 blade [bled] (n.) 刀片

🎧 'Take cover before the Indians return', shouted Hawkeye.

Hawkeye, Heyward and the Mohicans hid among the rocks. The Indians shouted and cried in anger. They fired their rifles and Chingachgook fired back. Bullets[1] whizzed[2] over the men's heads.

'Let them use up their gunpowder', said Hawkeye. 'Uncas, be careful. Don't waste[3] your bullets.'

'Uncas saved my life', said Heyward. He shook the hand of the Mohican. 'Thank you, Uncas', he said, 'I owe you a great debt[4].'

'Uncas, go to the canoe', said Hawkeye. 'Bring our gunpowder. We need it.'

But it was too late. There was an Indian in the water, pushing the boat down the river. Hawkeye aimed his gun and pressed the trigger. The gun did not fire.

'Too late', said Hawkeye. 'The gunpowder is finished and we cannot get any more from the boat.'

The Indian shouted in triumph. From the woods, Hawkeye and the others heard the laughs and shouts of the other Indians.

'What can we do now?' said Heyward. 'What will happen to us?'

Hawkeye pointed to his head. 'We will lose our scalps', he said.

'No', said Cora, 'you do not have to die. Go! You are brave men. You have done enough. Now leave us and save yourselves.'

'Perhaps the river will carry us to safety', said Hawkeye.

'Then try', said Cora.

'What will we say to Munro when he asks about his children? Will we say that we let the Indians kill them?'

'Tell him that you left us to get help. Tell him that if he comes quickly, he can save us.'

Hawkeye and the Mohicans spoke in Delaware[5]. Chingachgook listened carefully, then he put his knife and tomahawk in his belt, and moved silently to the edge of the rocks. A moment later he dropped into the water, and disappeared from sight. Hawkeye held Cora's hand for a moment. Then he put his rifle down on the rocks and followed Chingachgook into the water.

Cora looked at Uncas.

'Uncas will stay', said the Mohican.

'No. You must go. You are a kind and generous man', said Cora. 'Go to my father. Help him to buy our freedom. Please go. I want you to go.'

Uncas crossed the rocks. He looked at Cora one more time. There was an expression of great sadness on his face. Then he dropped into the river.

Cora turned to look at Heyward. 'You must follow them', she told him. 'The worst thing that can happen to us is that we will die. Everyone has to die sooner or later.'

'There are evils[6] worse than death,' said Heyward. 'I will give up[7] my life to save you from these.'

DECISIONS

★ Why did Cora send Hawkeye and the Mohicans away?
★ Did she make the right decision?
★ Have you ever had to make a difficult decision? What happened?

1 bullet ['bʊlɪt] (n.) 子彈
2 whiz [hwɪz] (v.) 颼颼掠過
3 waste [west] (v.) 浪費
4 I owe you a great debt 我欠你一個大人情

5 Delaware ['dɛləwɛr] (n.) 美國一原住民語言
6 evil ['ivl] (n.) 惡事
7 give up 放棄

Cora did not argue with Heyward. Alice was weeping[1]. Cora put her arm around her sister and guided her into the cave.

1 weep [wip] (v.) 哭泣

CHAPTER 6

There was no sign of the Indians. Heyward helped Gamut into the cave.

'Pray that the Indians do not find us', said Heyward.

The air inside the cave was fresh. Gamut's head still hurt, but he felt like singing.

'The Indians may hear us', said Cora.

'Let him sing', said Heyward. 'They won't hear his voice because of the waterfall. Anyway, it will make us all feel better.'

Gamut sang loudly and joyfully. But then there was a yell from outside the cave.

'They've found the body of one of their men. We are still safe', said Heyward.

Each time he heard a shout and a scream, Heyward thought the Indians had found their hiding place. The Indians were shouting out words that he could recognize.

'What are they saying?' whispered Cora.

'La Longue Carabine', said Heyward. 'It's French and it means "The Long Rifle". It's the name they call Hawkeye. They've found his gun and they think he is dead.'

The Indians were talking in excited voices.

'They are looking for his body', said Heyward. 'That means that our friends have escaped. If they reach General Webb, we will have help in less than two hours.'

The Indians continued their search. The women sat close together, trembling[1]. Soon they could hear the Indians clearly in the next cave.

'Don't move', whispered Heyward.

Alice started to cry.

'Hush[2]', said Cora and she held her sister more tightly.

There was a cry from outside. The Indians ran out of the cave.

'They've found another body', said Heyward.

They all waited. The Indians did not come back.

'They've gone, Cora', said Heyward. 'Alice, they've gone back to their camp and we are safe!'

Alice relaxed. The color returned to her face. She started to speak, but then she froze[3] and turned pale again. She was looking towards the entrance of the cave with an expression of terror on her face. An Indian was staring into the cave. His face was covered in warpaint. Heyward recognized the face of Magua.

Magua did not see Heyward and the others immediately. Then his eyes adjusted to the darkness inside the cave and the expression on his face changed. He looked triumphant. Heyward fired his gun, but Magua vanished.

Heyward ran to the entrance of the cave. He saw Magua running along a narrow rock. Then he disappeared again. For a moment there was silence. Then Magua yelled his war cry and all the other Indians replied with terrifying cries and screams.

The Indians attacked the cave from both sides. There was no chance of escape.

The Indians dragged[4] Heyward, Gamut and the women from the cave. They surrounded them, hooting[5] and whooping[6] in triumph.

FEAR

★ Have you ever felt afraid? What were you afraid of?
★ What happened?
★ What kind of things make you feel afraid? Make a list.
  Compare your list with your partner's.

1 tremble [ˈtrɛmbl̩] (v.) 發抖
2 hush [hʌʃ] (int.) 噓；別作聲
3 freeze [friz] (v.) 嚇得呆住；戰慄
4 drag [dræg] (v.) 拖著行進
5 hoot [hut] (v.) 發出像貓頭鷹的叫聲；發出表示不滿的叫喊
6 whoop [hwup] (v.) 高喊；吶喊

Heyward came face-to-face with Magua. This man had been their guide. Now they were his prisoners. Heyward felt angry.

'My men want the life of the hunter, Hawkeye, The Long Rifle', said Magua.

Heyward noticed that Magua's shoulder was bandaged with leaves.

'Hawkeye has gone', said Heyward.

Magua smiled, 'When the white man dies, he thinks he is at peace, but the red men know how to torture[1] the ghosts of their enemies. Where is Hawkeye's body? Let the Hurons see his scalp.'

'He isn't dead. He has escaped.'

Magua shook his head. 'Did he fly away like a bird, or maybe he swam away like a fish? Do you think we are fools?' he said.

'He's not a fish, but he can certainly swim.'

'And why did the white chief stay?' asked Magua. 'Do you want to lose your scalp?'

'White men don't desert[2] their women. They aren't cowards.'

Magua scowled[3]. 'Can the Mohicans swim, too', said Magua, 'as well as crawl in the bushes? Where are Big Snake Chingachgook, and Bounding Deer?'

'Who is Bounding Deer?' asked Heyward.

'Uncas', said Magua.

'Both of them floated down the river.'

The Hurons didn't understand what Heyward was saying. They looked at Magua and waited patiently for him to explain. Magua said a few words and pointed to the river. The Hurons gave a yell of disappointment. One of the Hurons grabbed Alice's hair and waved[4] his knife around her head. Heyward tried to stop him but his hands were tied together. Alice screamed in terror.

---

1 torture [ˈtɔrtʃɚ] (v.) 折磨
2 desert [dɪˈzɝt] (v.) 遺棄
3 scowl [skaʊl] (v.) 拉下臉；顯出怒容
4 wave [wev] (v.) 揮著

'Stay calm, Alice', he said. 'They won't hurt you. They're trying to frighten you.'

The Hurons shouted and pointed in the direction of General Webb's camp. They pushed their prisoners into the canoe and took them across the rapids[5] to the south bank of the river. There other Hurons were waiting with the horses. Most of the Indians left and disappeared into the woods. Magua remained with six Hurons and the prisoners. The women and Gamut rode the horses. The rest went on foot. The whole party now headed towards the south in an opposite direction from Fort William Henry.

When Cora passed trees and bushes, she grabbed twigs[6] and broke them, leaving a trail for Hawkeye. When no one was looking, she dropped her glove. But then one of the Hurons stopped her horse. He handed[7] her the lost glove and gave her a menacing[8] look.

---

5 rapid [ˈræpɪd] (n.) 急流
6 twig [twɪɡ] (n.) 細枝
7 hand [hænd] (v.) 遞給
8 menacing [ˈmɛnɪsɪŋ] (a.) 險惡的

CHAPTER 7

When the Hurons stopped to rest, Magua called Heyward. 'Go to the dark-haired daughter of Munro, and say, "Magua waits to speak".'

Heyward went to get Cora.

'What does he want?' she asked.

'I don't know', said Heyward, 'perhaps he wants something from your father.'

When she was alone with Magua, Cora asked: 'What does Magua want from the daughter of Munro?' She spoke calmly even though her heart beat fast. 'Magua must release[1] my sister. If my father loses both his daughters, it will send him to his grave. Surely this will give Magua no satisfaction.'

'Your sister can go', said Magua, 'in exchange for your promise.'

'What must I promise?' asked Cora.

'When Magua left his people, they gave his wife to another chief. Now he will return to the graves of his tribe, on the shores of the great lake. The daughter of the English chief will follow him, and live in his wigwam[2] forever.'

Cora shivered[3]. She was filled with disgust[4] by this proposal[5], but she did not show Magua her feelings.

'Does Magua want to share his home with a wife he does not love, a wife who is of a different nation and color? It is better to take the gold of Munro, and use it to buy the heart of a Huron woman.'

Magua did not reply. He stared at Cora's face for a long time. She looked away, embarrassed.

Magua spoke to her with hate in his voice. 'The daughter of Munro will carry Magua's water, she will work in his fields, and cook his meat. This way Magua's knife will touch Munro's heart.'

'You want to hurt my father!' cried Cora. 'Only a monster could plan this kind of revenge.'

Magua smiled. 'Go', he said, 'go back to your sister. The Hurons are preparing many tortures for you. Go and look.'

Cora saw that the Hurons had prepared bonfires[6] and sharp wooden stakes[7]. They had bent two young trees to the ground and intended to tie Heyward between them. Cora was horrified.

1 release [rɪˈlis] (v.) 釋放
2 wigwam [ˈwɪɡwɑm] (n.) 印第安人用樹皮或獸皮覆蓋而成的棚屋
3 shiver [ˈʃɪvɚ] (v.) 發抖；打顫
4 disgust [dɪsˈɡʌst] (n.) 嫌惡
5 proposal [prəˈpozḷ] (n.) 提議
6 bonfire [ˈbɑnˌfaɪr] (n.) 營火
7 stake [stek] (n.) 木樁

'What does the daughter of Munro say now?' said Magua. 'Is she still too good to live in Magua's wigwam? Does she want to become food for the wolves?'

'What does he mean, Cora?' said Heyward.

'Nothing', said Cora. 'He is a savage. He doesn't understand what he is doing. We must pray for him and pardon him.'

Magua pointed to Alice. 'Look! The child is crying! She is too young to die! Send her back to Munro. She can comb[1] his grey hair.'

Alice looked at her sister. 'What does he mean?', she said. 'Can I go home to father?'

'Alice', said Cora, 'the Huron will let us live, but on condition that I agree . . .' She stopped, unable to speak.

'No, no, no', cried Alice. 'It's better for us to die as we have lived, together.'

'Then die!' shouted Magua, and he threw his tomahawk with violence at Alice. It flew through the air past Heyward, and cut off a length of Alice's hair before it landed in a tree above her head. With all his strength Heyward broke the bonds[2] that tied his hands.

One of the Hurons was aiming his tomahawk at Alice. Heyward rushed at him. The two men fought each other and fell to the ground. The Indian slipped out of[3] Heyward's hands. He put his knee on Heyward's chest so that Heyward could not move. Then Heyward saw a knife in the Indian's hand. He heard the crack of a rifle. He saw the Indian's expression change, and the man fell dead by his side.

---

1 comb [kom] (v.) 用梳子梳理（頭髮）
2 bonds [bɑndz] (n.) （作複數形）鐐；銬；束縛
3 slip out of 溜走
4 howl [haʊl] (v.) 嗥叫；怒吼

The Hurons howled[4] when they saw their companion die. 'The Long Rifle', they shouted. 'The Long Rifle has come.'

The air filled with more whoops and yells. Hawkeye ran from the bushes. He picked up his old rifle and swung[5] it in the air like a club[6]. He smashed it over the heads of the Indians who were standing in his way. A figure ran past him and jumped into the middle of the Hurons. It was Uncas, whirling[7] his tomahawk and slashing[8] his knife at the Hurons. Another Indian joined him, and attacked the Hurons ferociously[9].

The shocked Indians screamed out two names: 'Bounding Deer', 'Big Snake', and they ran from the Mohicans. Magua took out his knife and rushed with a loud whoop at Chingachgook. The Hurons fought hand-to-hand with the Mohicans and Hawkeye. Uncas jumped on one of the Hurons and smashed[10] his tomahawk into the other's head. Heyward grabbed a knife and joined the fighting. The men fought each other with the fury[11] of a whirlwind[12] until the Hurons were dead or dying.

Chingachgook and Magua struggled in a cloud. They exchanged blows[13] and fell to the ground, close to the edge of some rocks. Hawkeye and Heyward watched the fight, unable to help. Hawkeye aimed his rifle and then lowered it again. Heyward tried to grab Magua's legs without success. Uncas was ready to stab[14] Magua with his knife, but the two Indians rolled over and over in the dust. At last Chingachgook stabbed Magua with his knife. Magua fell backwards into the dust. Chingachgook jumped to his feet and shouted in triumph.

---

5 swing [swɪŋ] (v.) 揮舞；擺動
6 club [klʌb] (n.) 棍棒
7 whirl [hwɜl] (v.) 旋轉
8 slash [slæʃ] (v.) 揮擊
9 ferociously [fəˋroʃəslɪ] (adv.) 兇猛地
10 smash [smæʃ] (v.) 猛擲

11 fury [ˋfjʊrɪ] (n.) 猛烈
12 whirlwind [ˋwɜl͵wɪnd] (n.) 旋風；旋流
13 blow [blo] (n.) 擊毆
14 stab [stæb] (v.) 戳；刺入

'Victory to the Mohicans', cried Hawkeye and he lifted up his rifle to smash it onto Magua's head. But, just at that moment, Magua rolled out of the way and over the edge of the rocks. He jumped into the centre of some bushes. The Mohicans chased after him.

'Let him go', shouted Hawkeye.

The Mohicans hesitated[1] then stopped.

'Let him go', said Hawkeye. 'He has no weapons. He can't do any harm now. He's like a rattlesnake[2] without fangs[3]. Just make sure the others are dead.'

Alice cried in Cora's arms. 'We're safe!' she said. 'We can go back to father. Thank goodness.'

'How did you get here so soon, my friend?' Heyward asked Hawkeye.

'We didn't go to the fort', said Hawkeye. 'We followed you and waited for our chance to attack.'

Uncas made a fire and prepared the food left by the Hurons.

'Let's eat', said Hawkeye. 'We have a long journey ahead of us.'

Hawkeye and the Mohicans ate in silence, and then drank from a nearby spring[4].

'It's time to go', said Hawkeye.

The two sisters mounted[5] their horses. Heyward and Gamut followed on foot. Hawkeye walked in front and the Mohicans at the back. They proceeded towards the north along narrow paths. They left the bodies of the Hurons behind them.

1 hesitate [ˈhɛzə‚tet] (v.) 躊躇；猶豫
2 rattlesnake [ˈrætḷ‚snek] (n.) 響尾蛇
3 fang [fæŋ] (n.) 毒牙
4 spring [sprɪŋ] (n.) 泉
5 mount [maʊnt] (v.) 爬上；騎上

CHAPTER 8

 After many hours the group arrived at an old battleground.

'I fought the Maquas here with Chingachgook', said Hawkeye. 'It was the first time I ever killed anyone. We can shelter here.'

They pushed through the bushes and came to an open space. In the centre was a hill and on the hill there was an old deserted[1] building. Alice and Cora dismounted[2], and relaxed in the coolness of the evening. The men went to look at the building.

'Not many people know about this place', Hawkeye told them. 'I was very young at that time. The sight of blood was new to me. We were trapped here for forty days and forty nights, with the Indians screaming for our blood. I buried the dead with my own hands under the small hill where you are sitting now.'

Heyward and the sisters stood up immediately.

'Don't be afraid. They are dead,' said Hawkeye, 'and they are harmless[3].' He smiled sadly at Heyward and the women.

The Mohicans cleared the leaves from a spring so that they could drink its water. In the old building, they put dried leaves on the floor for the sisters to sleep on.

'Chingachgook will be our guard. Let us all sleep', said Hawkeye.

The Mohican sat upright[4] and was motionless[5] in the darkness. He heard every tiny sound, from the breathing of the sisters to the leaves rustling[6] in the night breeze.

Heyward fell into a deep sleep. A light tap[7] on his shoulder woke him up. He sprang[8] to his feet immediately.

'Who's there?' he said. 'Friend or enemy?'

'Friend.' It was the voice of Chingachgook. He pointed to the moon. 'Moon comes', he said, 'White man's fort is far away. It is time to go.'

Hawkeye guided the party safely through the woods. He seemed to be at home in these surroundings. The path became uneven as they came closer to the mountains.

Suddenly, Hawkeye stopped.

'Be careful here', he whispered. 'There is an army camped close by.'

'We must be near to Fort William Henry', said Heyward.

'Be silent and keep close to me', said Hawkeye.

They had only gone a short distance when they saw someone coming towards them.

'Get your weapons ready, my friends', said Hawkeye.

A voice spoke in French, 'Who's there?'

DANGER

★ Who do you think is coming towards the party?
★ Why does Hawkeye tell everyone to get their weapons ready?
★ Have you ever been in a dangerous situation?
★ How did you feel? Describe to a partner.
★ Invent a dangerous situation and tell a partner.

1 deserted [dɪˈzɝtɪd] (a.) 無人居住的
2 dismount [dɪsˈmaʊnt] (v.) 下馬；下車
3 harmless [ˈhɑrmlɪs] (a.) 無害的
4 upright [ˈʌpˌraɪt] (adv.) 挺直地
5 motionless [ˈmoʃənləs] (a.) 不動的
6 rustling [ˈrʌslɪŋ] (n.) 沙沙聲
7 tap [tæp] (n.) 輕拍
8 spring [sprɪŋ] (v.) 跳；彈起

 Hawkeye did not answer.

'Who's there?' repeated the same voice.

This time Heyward answered in French. He gave the password. 'France'.

'Are you an officer of the king?' asked the guard.

'I certainly am', said Heyward in perfect French. 'I have with me the daughters of Colonel Munro. They are my prisoners and I'm taking them to the general.'

The soldier directed Heyward and the women to the camp. A few moments later they heard a long groan[1] from behind them.

'What was that?' said Alice.

'You should ask, "Who was that?"' said Hawkeye.

Heyward looked around and noticed that Chingachgook was missing. They heard another groan and then the sound of something heavy falling into the water.

Chingachgook came out of the bushes a few minutes later. Hawkeye quickly led his party to high rocky ground. From the edge of the rocks they could see the shore of the lake and the buildings of Fort William Henry. Close to the fort was an army camp.

'Look towards the south', said Hawkeye. 'Do you see the smoke rising from the woods? The enemy is in that direction.'

On the western bank of the lake, they could see the white tents and military equipment of a huge army camp.

'How many men do you think they have?' asked Heyward.

'Maybe ten thousand', said Hawkeye.

As they watched, they heard the roar of cannons[2] coming from the valley and echoing along the eastern hills. The group continued towards the plain that was opposite one side of the fort. The lake was covered by a thick fog. Suddenly they heard the words, 'Who goes there?' It was another of the French guards.

'Move on', whispered Hawkeye.

More voices called out in French, 'Who goes there?'

'Move on', repeated Heyward. Then he called out, 'It's me'.

'Me? Who?' was the reply.

'A friend of France', said Heyward.

'You're an enemy of France', shouted one of the French soldiers.

Many voices shouted, then came the order, 'Fire!'

Fifty guns exploded into the fog. Bullets flew through the air, but Hawkeye's party was moving in a different direction.

---

1 groan [gron] (n.) 呻吟聲；哼聲
2 cannon [ˈkænən] (n.) 大砲

'Fire back!' said Hawkeye. 'They will think it is an attack and they will retreat[1] and wait for help.'

The plan was good but it did not work. When the French heard the shots, they sent more men.

'We should run for our lives', said Heyward. 'Soon the whole army will be here.'

A light flashed. Several cannons fired across the plain.

'Let's run towards the fort', said Hawkeye.

Hawkeye and his party ran in the direction of the fort. Uncas took Cora's arm and guided her. They could hear the soldiers following them. Then, they heard a voice inside the fort.

'Get ready. Wait until you see the enemy. Then fire!'

Alice recognized the voice immediately.

'Father! Father!' she cried. 'It's Alice. Save us! Save your daughters!'

'Hold your fire', shouted Munro. 'It's my daughter! Quickly, open the gates. Don't fire. Use your swords.'

A group of soldiers rushed out of the fort. Heyward joined them in the fight against the French soldiers. For an instant, Cora and Alice stood alone, trembling. But then an older officer ran towards the girls and put his arms around them and hugged them. Tears rolled[2] down his face, and in a Scottish accent, he shouted, 'Thank you, God, for saving my daughters!'

---

1 retreat [rɪˋtrit] (v.) 撤退
2 roll [rol] (v.) 滾動
3 siege [sidʒ] (n.) 圍攻
4 reinforcements [ˌriɪnˋforsmənts] (n.) (作複數形) 援軍
5 matter [ˋmætə] (n.) 問題

CHAPTER 9

The siege[3] continued over the following days. Colonel Munro did his best to fight off the French attacks. The woods around the fort were filled with Montcalm's Indians, and there was no hope of escape for the soldiers. General Webb sent no reinforcements[4]. It seemed as though he had forgotten about the men at the fort.

Heyward had not seen Cora and Alice since their terrible journey together, but on the fifth day he met them walking along the walls of the fort with their father. They looked rested and fresh.

'Major Heyward', said Cora. 'We didn't get the chance to thank you for saving us.'

'Major Heyward', said Munro, 'I need your help in another matter[5].'

'How can I help?' said Heyward.

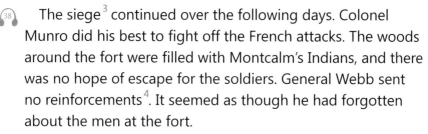

HELP

★ When you are in trouble do you ask for help?
★ Who do you ask?
★ Do you offer to help people?
★ Or do others often ask for your help?
★ Think of a situation in which you asked for help or you were of help to someone. Describe it.

Munro spoke to Heyward and ten minutes later the young officer was on his way to Montcalm's camp. A French officer accompanied him to the commander's tent. French officers, Indian chiefs from different tribes and warriors surrounded the French commander. Heyward stopped when he saw the evil face of Magua staring at him. Montcalm greeted Heyward.

'I am very happy to welcome you in place of your superior Colonel Munro', he said.

Heyward bowed and Montcalm, after pausing for a moment, said, 'Do you know the strength of our army, Major Heyward?'

'We do not have an exact number', said Heyward. 'The highest figure we have is not more than twenty thousand men.'

The Frenchman studied Heyward's face carefully. The number that Heyward gave was double[1] the actual number. Montcalm continued, 'So', he said, 'you have come to discuss the terms of your surrender[2].'

'I think', said Heyward, 'that you do not know the strength of Fort William Henry.'

'I believe the fort has just two thousand, three hundred men', said Montcalm.

'The fort is strong and well-situated on the shore of the lake', said Heyward. 'There is also a powerful army just a few hours' march from here.'

---

1 double ['dʌbḷ] (a.) 兩倍的
2 surrender [sə'rɛndɚ] (n.) 投降

'About six or eight thousand men', said Montcalm. 'But General Webb thinks it is better to keep them at home than to send them here.'

When their discussion ended, Heyward left. He was impressed by the hospitality[1] and good manners of Montcalm, but he knew nothing more about the real strength of his army.

MANNERS

★ Are good manners important in our society today? Give some examples of 'good manners' and 'bad manners'. Discuss with your partner what you normally do in these situations:
1. You are at the back of a crowd of people waiting to be served in a shop.
2. You have a comfortable seat on the bus when an older person gets on.
3. You want to speak to someone but the door of their room is shut.

At the fort, Heyward told Munro about his meeting.

'General Webb is sending his army to help us', said Munro. 'I will never surrender the fort.'

The discussion of a surrender was closed. Heyward took the opportunity to discuss another matter.

'I have a request', said Heyward.

'I think I know what it is', said Munro.

'Will you allow me the honor of being your son?' said Heyward.

'You speak very clearly, Heyward', said Munro. 'Did you also speak clearly to my daughter?'

'I did not', said Heyward, 'You trusted me and I did not abuse[2] that trust.'

'You are a gentleman then, Major Heyward, but Cora is too intelligent to need the protection of her father.'

'Cora?' said Heyward.

'Yes, Cora. We are talking about your interest in Miss Munro, I think.'

'I . . . I don't think I mentioned her name', said Heyward.

'Well, then who did you want to marry?' said Munro.

'You have another child who is just as lovely.'

'Alice?' said Munro.

'You should know something about my background', said Munro. 'I come from a noble Scottish family, but we were not very wealthy. When I was about your age, I met Alice Graham, the daughter of a local lord. I proposed marriage, but her father would not agree. I joined the army and left to serve my king overseas[3]. I visited many lands and I fought in many wars. Then my duty took me to the West Indies. There I met my wife, the mother of Cora. She was the daughter of a gentleman, but her ancestors had been slaves. In many places people think that the children of slaves are inferior to themselves.'

1 hospitality [ˌhɑspɪˈtælətɪ] (n.) 友好
2 abuse [əˈbjuz] (v.) 濫用
3 overseas [ˈovɚˌsiz] (adv.) 在國外

'Unfortunately that is true', said Heyward.

'Perhaps you think that my daughter Cora is not good enough for you', said Munro.

'I hope I will never be guilty of such prejudice', said Heyward. 'I fell in love with the sweetness and beauty of your younger daughter Alice.'

'Alice is the image of[1] her mother', said Munro. 'When Cora's mother died, I returned to Scotland and I found my sweetheart[2] still unmarried. In those twenty years she had thought of me, but I had married someone else and forgotten her. When I returned, she forgave[3] me and became my wife.'

'And she became the mother of Alice?' said Heyward.

'She did, indeed,' said Munro, 'but she was only my wife for one year before she died.' As Munro spoke, tears rolled down his face. 'Let's change the subject', he said. 'We must discuss Montcalm.'

Munro agreed to meet the French commander accompanied by Heyward. As before, Montcalm was courteous[4] and welcoming. He spoke in French and Heyward translated.

'Please tell Colonel Munro this. He and his men have fought us gallantly[5]. Now it is time for them to give up[6]. My army is stronger. It is impossible to defeat us.'

'I know that the French army is strong', replied Munro, 'but my king also has many faithful soldiers.'

'Fortunately for us, they are not here', said Montcalm in English.

'I see the commander knows English well', said Heyward.

'I ask your pardon[7], monsieur[8]', said Montcalm. 'There is a great difference between understanding and speaking a foreign language. Please continue to translate.'

FOREIGN LANGUAGES

★ How many languages can you speak?

★ Is it difficult to learn a foreign language?

★ What does Montcalm mean when he says that 'there is a great difference between understanding and speaking a foreign language'?

Then he added, 'From these hills we can watch your activities so I know exactly the strength of your army.'

'Can your telescope see as far as the Hudson River?' asked Munro. 'Will you see the army of General Webb arriving?'

1 the image of 長得相像
2 sweetheart [ˋswit͵hɑrt] (n.) 心上人
3 forgive [fəˋgɪv] (v.) 原諒
4 courteous [ˋkɝtjəs] (a.) 謙恭有禮的
5 gallantly [ˋgæləntlɪ] (adv.) 勇敢地
6 give up 放棄
7 pardon [ˋpɑrdn̩] (n.) 原諒
8 monsieur [məˋsjɝ] (n.) 〔法語〕先生；閣下

'Let General Webb speak for himself', said Montcalm, giving Munro a letter.

Munro did not wait for Heyward to translate Montcalm's words. As he read the letter, tears filled his eyes. The letter fell from his hand. He looked like a man who had lost all hope. Heyward picked up the letter and read it.

In the letter General Webb advised Munro to surrender. He was not going to send a single soldier to help them.

'The letter is genuine[1]', said Heyward, 'this is Webb's signature[2].'

'He has betrayed me', said Munro.

'We still command the fort', said Heyward. 'We still have our honor.'

'I thank you', said Munro. 'You have reminded me of my duty. We will return and dig our graves inside the fort.'

'Messieurs', said Montcalm, 'listen to my terms[3] before you leave. I promise you that your surrender will be honorable[4].'

Munro thought for a moment. 'Heyward, make the arrangements[5] for our surrender with General Montcalm', he said. 'In my old age I have lived to see two things. I have seen an Englishman who is too afraid to help a friend, and I have seen a Frenchman who is too honest to profit from his success.'

When Munro walked back to the fort, everyone knew he brought bad news. He never recovered from the shock of this defeat. Heyward arranged the terms of the surrender and Munro signed the treaty[6]. He agreed to surrender the fort in the morning. The army could keep its weapons, its flag, its belongings[7] and, consequently, its honor.

1 genuine [ˈdʒɛnjuɪn] (a.) 真跡的
2 signature [ˈsɪgnətʃə] (n.) 署名
3 terms [tɝmz] (n.) 條件
4 honorable [ˈɑnərəbl] (a.) 光榮的
5 make the arrangements 安排
6 treaty [ˈtritɪ] (n.) 合約
7 belongings [bəˈlɔŋɪŋz] (n.) 擁有物

CHAPTER 10

 Montcalm stepped out of his tent into the cold morning air.
'Who goes there?' shouted one of the guards.
'General Montcalm.'
'Morning, sir', said the guard. 'And enjoy your walk.'
Montcalm walked toward the west side of Fort William Henry.
There was a sound. It was Magua and he was pointing a rifle at
Montcalm's head.

'What are you doing here?' said Montcalm. 'The fighting is
over.'

The Indian replied in French. 'The warriors have no scalps', he
said, 'and the pale faces make friends.'

Magua disappeared and Montcalm returned to the camp.

Trumpets sounded in the French camp. It was the day of
the surrender. Outside the fort the French soldiers stood to
attention in the sunshine. Inside the fort, there was a different
scene. Women and children prepared to leave. Soldiers lined
up[1] in silence. Munro stood sadly in front of his men.

Cora and Alice watched the soldiers march out of the fort.
At the same time French grenadiers[2] took control of the fort's
gates. As the British soldiers marched away with Heyward in
front, Cora heard a familiar cry. Suddenly almost a hundred
Indians seemed to appear from nowhere. In the middle of this
group Cora saw Magua. He was shouting to the Hurons and
giving them instructions.

   A crowd of women came out of the fort. One of them, a mother carrying a baby, was wearing a brightly colored shawl. A Huron stepped forward and tried to take the shawl from her. The woman quickly wrapped it around her child. The Indian pulled the baby from her. The shawl dropped to the ground and another Huron grabbed it. The woman screamed in terror.

At that moment, Magua placed his hands around his mouth and gave the Huron war cry. At this signal, more than two thousand Indians rushed out of the forest. The Indians were wild and angry. They wanted the scalps of their enemies. Blood flowed like a river. The soldiers tried to fight the Indians but they had no bullets in their guns.

Alice and Cora watched helplessly. Gamut stayed by their side. Around them they heard the shrieks and screams of the injured and the dying. Alice saw her father moving through the crowds of Indians towards the French camp. The Hurons waved their spears at Munro but he pushed them aside. They did not dare to hurt someone so important.

---

1 line up 排成行列
2 grenadier [ˌɡrɛnəˈdɪr] (n.) 英國近衛步兵團的士兵

'Father! Father! We are here!' shrieked Alice. Munro did not hear her. Alice dropped to the ground in a faint. Cora tried to revive[1] her.

'Let us take a chance and run', said Gamut.

'No, you go', said Cora, looking at her sister. 'Save yourself.'

Gamut stood up and started to sing. His voice was powerful and the Indians could hear him above the noise of the battle. More than one Indian rushed towards them with the intention of taking their scalps. The sight and sound of Gamut singing made them change their minds. They left him and the women unharmed.

The sound of Gamut's voice reached Magua's ears. He ran towards Gamut and the women.

'Come', he said to Cora.

'Get away from me', cried Cora.

The Indian laughed and showed her the blood on his hands. 'It is red', he said, 'but it comes from white veins!'

'You're a monster!' screamed Cora. 'You caused this to happen.'

'Magua is a great chief!' said the Indian. 'Will the dark-haired woman come to his tribe?'

'Never!' said Cora. 'You can kill me now and have your revenge.'

Magua hesitated for a moment. Then he picked Alice up in his arms and ran with her towards the woods.

'No, stop!' cried Cora, running after him. 'Let her go', she screamed.

Magua ignored her. Gamut followed Cora, singing at the top of his voice. The two of them crossed the plain in this way, passing the wounded, the dead, and people who were running for their lives.

1 revive [rɪˋvaɪv] (v.) 使甦醒過來

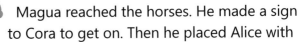 Magua reached the horses. He made a sign to Cora to get on. Then he placed Alice with her sister on the same horse. He led the horse away towards the forest. Gamut mounted another horse and followed.

They traveled for a long time, and then they reached the flat surface of a mountain top. From there they could see the plain outside the fort. Bodies covered the ground. The killing continued and in the distance Alice and Cora could hear the cries of the wounded. Soon they could only hear the whoops of the Indians who were celebrating their work.

Three days after the massacre, the area around the fort was silent and still. The Indians had gone. Their camp was empty. The fort was a smoldering[1] ruin[2].

Just before the sun set, five men – Hawkeye, the two Mohicans, Munro and Heyward – came out of the forest and walked towards the fort. They looked at the bodies, praying that Alice and Cora were not among the dead. Uncas tore something from a bush and waved it at the others. It was a piece of Cora's green veil. It was a tiny clue[3] that the women were still alive.

---

1 smoldering [ˈsmoldərɪŋ] (a.) 悶燒的
2 ruin [ˈruɪn] (n.) 廢墟；斷垣殘壁
3 clue [klu] (n.) 線索
4 whistle [ˈhwɪsl] (n.) 笛子

'My child!' cried Munro, 'give me my child!'

'Uncas will try,' said the Mohican.

Chingachgook pointed to a footprint.

'Here are the tracks', said Heyward. 'They are captives of the Indians.'

'We will find them, I promise you', said Hawkeye. 'This is a moccasin track. What do you think, Uncas?'

The young Mohican studied the track.

'Magua', he said.

'Yes', Hawkeye agreed, 'Magua and the dark-haired woman were here.'

'What about Alice?' asked Heyward.

'There's no sign of her', said Hawkeye. He looked around at the trees and the bushes. 'There's something in that thorn bush', he said.

Uncas went to look and returned with Gamut's whistle[4].

'He's left us a clue', said Hawkeye. 'He's cleverer than I thought. Uncas, look for the preacher's footprints.'

As it grew dark, the men returned to the ruins of the old fort.

'Rest now', said Hawkeye. 'In the morning we will be fresh and ready to continue our search.'

CLUES

★ How do they know that Cora is still alive? Name three clues.

★ With a partner make a short treasure hunt. Write clues and test another pair.

CHAPTER 11

 'Follow me', said Hawkeye. 'Be careful to walk on the stones and on pieces of wood.'

The men did as Hawkeye told them.

'Now our trail will be difficult to follow', said Hawkeye. 'You can always find footprints on grass, but not on wood or stone. It's good that you left your boots at home. Your moccasins won't leave a print[1] and it's easier to walk in moccasins.'

On the shore of the lake Uncas pushed a canoe into the water, taking care not to leave marks in the sand. The men climbed into the canoe and the Mohicans paddled[2] it away from the fort.

The day dawned. They traveled across the lake and around many little islands. It was possible the Indians were still in the area. For this reason they had to travel in silence. Chingachgook pointed to a cloud that was rising into the sky from one of the islands.

'It's smoke from a fire', said Hawkeye.

By the northern shore of the island, they saw two canoes.

'They haven't seen us yet', said Hawkeye. 'Let's go.'

But before he had finished speaking they heard the crack of a rifle. The Hurons had seen them and ran to their canoes and pushed them into the water. Hawkeye and the Mohicans continued to paddle and their canoe moved forward swiftly[3].

'Keep this distance between our canoe and theirs', said Hawkeye. 'The bullets from their rifles cannot reach us.' He put down his paddle and aimed his rifle at the enemy.

He waited for their canoe to come into range[4], but before he could fire, another canoe appeared. The canoes raced each other through the water. The Hurons paddled as fast as they could to catch Hawkeye's canoe, but there was no opportunity for them to fire their guns.

'We're right in their firing line[5]', said Heyward.

Chingachgook gave the war-whoop of the Mohicans. The Hurons shouted out the names of Hawkeye and the Mohicans: 'Long Rifle!' 'Big Snake!' 'Bounding Deer!'

Hawkeye waved his rifle at the Hurons. The Indians answered back with bullets that hit the surface of the water. Hawkeye aimed at the Indians' canoe and fired. The Huron at the front of the first canoe fell backwards and dropped his gun into the water. Hawkeye and the Mohicans took advantage of the confusion and increased the distance between them and the Hurons' canoe.

The lake now grew wider, and on each side there were high mountains. They paddled now with more regular strokes[6]. It seemed to Heyward that for Hawkeye and the Mohicans the race was just like a game. Chingachgook directed the canoe towards the hills and the fort at Ticonderoga. The Hurons were far behind them. It looked as though they had given up the chase. Hawkeye kept watch for several hours until they reached the north side of the lake.

There were thick bushes at the side of the lake. This helped them to stay hidden. They continued their journey until Hawkeye said it was safe to land. They rested until it was evening. Then, they started their journey again and traveled silently towards the western shore. Uncas steered the canoe safely to the land.

---

1 print [prɪnt] (n.) 痕跡
2 paddle [ˈpædl] (v.) 用槳划
3 swiftly [ˈswɪftlɪ] (adv.) 迅速地
4 come into range 進入射程內
5 firing line 射程
6 stroke [strok] (n.) （船、游泳的）一划

PRACTICAL SKILLS

★ What practical skills have you got that would help you
survive outdoors like Hawkeye and the Mohicans? Tick (✓)
what you can do.

☐ Paddle a canoe   ☐ Swim
☐ Ride a horse   ☐ Make a fire
☐ Catch fish   ☐ Cook a meal
☐ Use a compass   ☐ Walk long distances
☐ Climb rocks   ☐ Get directions by reading the stars

The men carried the boat into the woods and hid it under
some tree branches. A few minutes later they picked up their
guns and supplies and started the next part of their journey.

CHAPTER 12

 Hawkeye led the party into a large, deserted area of land. Uncas studied the ground for tracks. Suddenly he pointed to a place where there was some fresh earth. It looked as though a large animal had recently passed that way.

'It's the trail', said Hawkeye. 'Uncas never misses any clues.'

By the middle of the afternoon they came to a place where Magua and his men had stopped to rest. The Hurons had made a fire and cooked some meat. The bones were scattered[1] around. Horses had eaten leaves from the trees. Someone had made a bed under the bushes. Heyward was sure Cora and Alice had slept there. The men moved forward in silence until they reached a hill.

'I can smell the Hurons', said Hawkeye. 'We are close to their camp. Chingachgook, go to the right of the hill. Uncas, go to the left and follow the stream. I will follow the trail. If there is a problem, croak three times like a crow.'

The Mohicans set off and Hawkeye continued with Heyward and Munro.

'Go to the edge of the wood', Hawkeye told Heyward. 'Wait for me there'.

1 scatter [ˈskætɚ] (v.) 散落

Hiding in the bushes, Heyward was amazed at what he saw. Over a hundred huts stood on the edge of the lake and in the water. Suddenly he heard the rustle of leaves. A short distance from him, he saw an Indian. Heyward did not move. The man had a painted face. Instead of looking fierce, Heyward thought he looked sad. He was studying the Indian when Hawkeye appeared at his side.

'Look', whispered Heyward, 'we've found their camp and here's one of them!'

Hawkeye stared at the Indian. 'This is not a Huron', he said, 'and he's wearing the clothes of a white man.'

Hawkeye crept behind the man. Heyward watched. Instead of grabbing him Hawkeye tapped the man on the shoulder and said in a low voice, 'What are you doing, my friend? Are you teaching the beavers[1] to sing now?'

'That's right', said the Indian, 'Why shouldn't they learn to sing, too?'

'Gamut!' said Heyward.

1 beaver ['bivə] (n.) 海狸；河狸

'Where are the women?' asked Hawkeye.

The men sat around Gamut waiting to hear his story.

'They are prisoners of the Hurons', said Gamut. 'But they are safe and in good health.'

'Both of them?' asked Heyward.

'Yes, both of them', said Gamut. 'They had a bad journey and little to eat but, apart from that, they are fine.'

'Thank goodness', said Munro. 'I'll soon get my children back.'

'Don't count on it', said Gamut. 'The Huron leader is like someone who has an evil spirit inside him. He and his men are out hunting today. They have left Alice with the Huron women a short distance from here. Cora is in another village on the other side of the mountains. The Indians there are on the side of Montcalm.'

'Why are you allowed to walk around freely?' asked Heyward.

'They seem to like my singing', said Gamut. 'They let me come and go as I please.'

'Good', said Hawkeye. 'Now go back and tell Alice we are coming.'

'I'll go with him', said Heyward. 'I'll pretend to be a madman or a fool. Just find me a disguise[1], change me, paint me . . . do anything.'

Chingachgook took on[2] the job of transforming[3] Heyward. The Mohican painted Heyward's face in the traditional way of the Indians. He gave him a happy, comical expression.

'Impressive!', said Hawkeye when Chingachgook had finished.

'How do I look?' asked Heyward.

'If you speak to them in French', said Hawkeye, 'they'll think you are a juggler[4] from Ticonderoga and that you come from a friendly tribe. Now, let's agree on our plan'.

---

1 disguise [dɪsˈɡaɪz] (n.) 偽裝   3 transform [trænsˈfɔrm] (v.) 改變
2 take on 接受   4 juggler [ˈdʒʌɡlɚ] (n.) 變戲法的人

CHAPTER 13

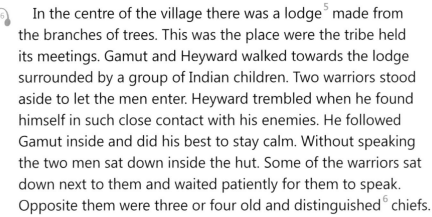

In the centre of the village there was a lodge[5] made from the branches of trees. This was the place were the tribe held its meetings. Gamut and Heyward walked towards the lodge surrounded by a group of Indian children. Two warriors stood aside to let the men enter. Heyward trembled when he found himself in such close contact with his enemies. He followed Gamut inside and did his best to stay calm. Without speaking the two men sat down inside the hut. Some of the warriors sat down next to them and waited patiently for them to speak. Opposite them were three or four old and distinguished[6] chiefs.

At last one of the chiefs spoke. 'We heard', he said, 'that the men of Canada were proud of their pale faces. Do they now paint their skin?'

'When an Indian chief comes among his white brothers', said Heyward, 'he takes off his buffalo robe and wears the shirt that they offer him. My brothers gave me paint and I am wearing it.'

DRESS

★ How do you dress in the following situations?
☐ meeting friends
☐ a family party
☐ in school
☐ an interview for a part-time job

---

5 lodge [lɑdʒ] (n.) 印第安人的棚屋
6 distinguished [dɪˈstɪŋgwɪʃt] (a.) 著名的;卓越的

The old chief made a gesture[1] of praise and his companions each gave an exclamation of pleasure. Heyward breathed more freely. He was about to speak when outside there was a high-pitched[2] yell.

The warriors immediately got up and left the lodge. Heyward and Gamut followed them. Outside the Indians were shouting and whooping loudly. A line of warriors came out of the woods towards the huts.

The warriors took out their knives, and waved them in the air. Then they stood in two lines with a path between the lines. Young boys took the tomahawks from their fathers' belts, and got into the line, copying their fathers' behavior. At the end of the line was a prisoner. He stood proudly, ready to meet his fate[3] like a hero. Someone shouted a signal. The Indians started to scream and shout loudly.

The prisoner ran between the lines of Indians as swiftly as a deer. Before anyone could hit him, he jumped over a row of children and ran towards the forest. The Indians chased him and nearly caught him. He ran in another direction and tried again to reach the forest. It was his last chance to escape.

A tall, powerful Huron ran towards him, waving his tomahawk in the air. Heyward put his foot out in front of the Indian. The man tripped[4] and fell and the prisoner ran for his life. Heyward looked up and saw him in front of the lodge standing quietly next to a small painted post[5]. It was a sacred[6] place. No one could touch him now until the Huron council decided his fate. For the first time Heyward saw the prisoner's face clearly. It was Uncas.

A warrior took Uncas by the arm, and led him into the lodge. The chiefs and the most important warriors entered and Heyward followed. Uncas stood calmly in the centre of the lodge.

'Mohican', the chief said to Uncas. 'You have proved that you are a man. I would ask you to eat with us, but he who eats with a Huron becomes his friend. Rest in peace until the morning. Then we will speak our last words.'

At that moment, an old squaw moved towards the prisoner. She danced slowly around Uncas waving a torch close to his face and mumbling an incantation[7]. Uncas stood proudly. He stared ahead and did not look at the woman.

BRAVERY

★ What person in the past do you consider to be brave?
★ What did they do?
★ Was there a time in your life when you were brave? What did you do?
★ Would you have been as brave as Uncas in the story?

1 gesture [ˈdʒɛstʃɚ] (n.) 手勢
2 high-pitched (a.) 聲音尖而高的
3 fate [fet] (n.) 命運
4 trip [trɪp] (v.) 跌倒
5 post [post] (n.) 柱子
6 sacred [ˈsekrɪd] (a.) 神聖的
7 incantation [ˌɪnkænˈteʃən] (n.) 咒文

Just then a dark figure appeared in the doorway. He entered and walked silently among the Indians. Then he sat down next to Heyward. Heyward glanced at the warrior and was filled with horror. The man sitting next to him was Magua.

Magua didn't notice Heyward. He looked at Uncas and shook his fist at him. The silver ornaments on his bracelets rattled. In a loud angry voice he said, 'Mohican, you will die!'

Then he stood up and whirled[1] his axe above his head. It flew through the air gleaming[2] in the torchlight and it sliced[3] through the hair on the top of Uncas's head.

Uncas stood still, looking his enemy in the eye.

'Take him away', said Magua. 'In the morning he will die.'

The young warriors immediately led Uncas out of the lodge. Magua followed them.

The chief finished smoking his pipe. Then he gave Heyward a sign to follow him.

'Come, stranger', he said. 'An evil spirit lives in the wife of one of my men. You are a medicine man[4]. You must frighten him away.'

They walked towards the foot of the nearby mountain and then along a narrow track. They started to cross a grassy[5] area when something large and black ran across their path. It was a bear. Heyward remembered that the Indians sometimes kept bears as pets, but he found it difficult not to worry. The bear followed them.

1 whirl [hwɜl] (v.) 旋轉
2 gleam [glim] (v.) 閃爍
3 slice [slaɪs] (v.) 切下；割去
4 medicine man 巫醫
5 grassy [ˈgræsɪ] (a.) 長滿草的

PETS

★ Like the Indians many people keep very unusual pets. Ask your
  partner which of the following they would like or not like to
  keep as a pet. Ask them to give reasons.
   ☐ a crocodile   ☐ a snake   ☐ a spider   ☐ a bear   ☐ a rat
★ What other unusual pets can you think of?
★ Which animals make the best pets?

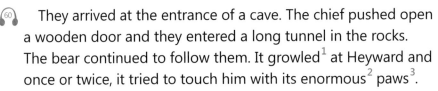

They arrived at the entrance of a cave. The chief pushed open
a wooden door and they entered a long tunnel in the rocks.
The bear continued to follow them. It growled[1] at Heyward and
once or twice, it tried to touch him with its enormous[2] paws[3].

There were many rooms inside the cave. The sick woman was
in one of these.

'Here it is more difficult for the evil spirits to find her', said
the chief.

A group of Indian women surrounded the sick woman's bed.
In the middle of them was Gamut. When Heyward saw the
woman, he knew immediately that he could not help her. She
seemed to be paralyzed[4].

Gamut began to sing a hymn. A voice that was half human
and half animal replied. Gamut looked around in alarm. He saw
the bear sitting in a dark corner of the cave. Its body swayed[5]
from side to side and it made low growling sounds as though
it was trying to copy Gamut's voice. Gamut was terrified and
stopped singing. He turned to Heyward and quickly whispered,
'Alice is waiting for you and she is nearby.' Then he ran from the
room.

The Huron chief sent the women away.

'Now let my brother show his power', he said, pointing to the sick woman.

Heyward pretended to recite[6] an incantation over the woman. A fierce growl from the bear interrupted him.

'The spirits are jealous', said the chief.

He faced the bear and spoke to it. 'Peace!', he said. Then he turned to Heyward and said, 'I will go.'

Heyward was left alone in the cave with a dying woman and a dangerous beast[7]. The bear walked towards Heyward and then sat in front of him. Heyward stared at the bear, expecting it to attack at any moment. The bear shook its whole body. It rubbed its face with its large paws. Suddenly its head seemed to fall to one side and in its place was the face of Hawkeye.

---

1 growl [graʊl] (v.) 咆哮
2 enormous [ɪˋnɔrməs] (a.) 巨大的
3 paw [pɔ] (n.) 爪子
4 paralyzed [ˋpærəˌlaɪzd] (a.) 癱瘓的
5 sway [swe] (v.) 搖擺
6 recite [rɪˋsaɪt] (v.) 吟誦
7 beast [bist] (n.) 野獸

CHAPTER 14

 'After we separated, Uncas and I went to the other camp',
said Hawkeye. 'Have you seen him?'

'The Hurons have him. They are going to kill him at sunrise',
said Heyward.

'I won't let the Hurons have him', said Hawkeye. He
continued his story. 'We met a party of Hurons. One of them
was a coward and ran away from us. Uncas followed him back
to his camp, but there the Indians captured him. I shot two of
the Hurons and came close to the village. Then, by chance, I
came across[1] one of the medicine men from the tribe. He was
dressing up in this bear skin so I decided to take it for myself.
Now, we have work to do. Do you know where Alice is?'

'I've looked all around the village', said Heyward, 'but I can't
find any trace of her.'

'You heard Gamut's words', said Hawkeye. 'She is nearby,
and she is waiting for you.'

The two men searched for her in the cave. Heyward saw a
light shining in the distance and went towards it. He found
a room full of objects stolen from Fort William Henry. In the
middle of the room Alice was sitting, pale and terrified, but as
beautiful as ever.

'I knew that you would never desert me', she cried.

Heyward knelt beside her. 'With the help of our friend
Hawkeye, we will escape from these savages,' he said, 'but
you must be brave.' He was interrupted by a light tap on his
shoulder. He jumped to his feet and turned. He was standing
face to face with Magua.

The Huron laughed scornfully[2] at the young couple.

'Magua is a great chief!' said the Indian. 'Now we will see how bravely a pale face[3] can laugh at tortures.'

Magua was about to leave when there was a loud growl. The figure of the bear appeared in the doorway. It swayed from side to side. Then suddenly it stretched its arms towards Magua and wrapped them tightly around his shoulders.

Magua struggled ferociously but Hawkeye pinned[4] his arms to his side. Heyward ripped[5] some leather strips off bundles of wood and used them to tie Magua's arms, legs and feet. He wrapped a cloth around his mouth to stop him from shouting. Then the men left him helpless and lying on his back in the cave.

'Now let's go quickly', said Hawkeye.

'Alice has fainted', said Heyward.

'Don't worry', said Hawkeye. 'Wrap her in Indian blankets. Carry her in your arms and follow. Leave the rest to me.'

1 come across 偶然碰見
2 scornfully [ˈskɔrnfəlɪ] (adv.) 輕蔑地
3 pale face 在此指白人
4 pin [pɪn] (v.) 壓住；按住
5 rip [rɪp] (v.) 撕；扯；剝

Hawkeye, in his bear disguise, walked outside. Heyward walked behind him. He found himself in the middle of twenty anxious[1] relatives and friends. The father of the sick woman and her husband approached.

'Has my brother driven away[2] the evil spirit?' said the father. 'What does he have in his arms?'

'Your child,' said Heyward. 'The spirit has left her and is closed inside the cave. I'm taking her to a distant place, where I will make her strong.'

'Go', said the Indian, 'We will wait outside the cave. If the spirit appears, we will beat him with sticks.'

The father and the woman's husband took out their tomahawks, and waited outside the cave. The women and children broke branches from the bushes, or picked up rocks, with the same intention. Heyward and Hawkeye disappeared quickly into the woods.

In the fresh air Alice revived. She was weak but she could walk.

'This path will lead you to the river', said Hawkeye. 'Follow it, then climb the hill on your right and you will find the village of the Delawares. Ask them for protection. You will be safe.'

'What about you?' said Heyward.

'Uncas, the last of the noble blood of the Mohicans is in the power of the Hurons', said Hawkeye. 'I must help him.'

Gamut was playing a tune on his whistle when the bear crept silently into his hut. Gamut froze. The bear shook his shaggy[3] fur and growled. Then it said, 'Put down that whistle, Gamut.'

'What are you?' cried Gamut in terror.

'Only me', said Hawkeye, taking off his furry bear head.

Gamut mumbled a prayer of thanks.

'Alice and Heyward are free', said Hawkeye. 'Now I need to find Uncas.'

'He's a prisoner', said Gamut.

'Lead[4] me to him,' said Hawkeye.

1 anxious [ˈæŋkʃəs] (a.) 焦急的
2 drive away 驅逐
3 shaggy [ˈʃægɪ] (a.) 長滿粗毛的
4 lead [lid] (v.) 帶領

The Huron warriors stepped aside to let Gamut enter the lodge. They saw that he was with a medicine man who was dressed as a bear. The warriors wanted to know what the medicine man was going to do. Hawkeye sat down and growled.

'The medicine man is afraid for his brothers', said Gamut. 'His breath will take away their courage. They must stand far away.'

The Hurons immediately moved back from the entrance of the lodge. Hawkeye and Gamut entered the building. Inside only a small fire lit the room. Uncas was in one corner. His feet and hands were tied. Uncas thought at first that his enemies had sent in a real bear. He closed his eyes and pressed his body against the wall of the hut. But the bear made a hissing noise like a snake. Uncas looked more closely at the animal.

'Hawkeye!' he said.

'Release him', Hawkeye told Gamut.

Hawkeye threw off his bear skin. He took out a long, glittering[1] knife and put it into Uncas's hands.

'The Hurons are outside,' he said. 'I will put on the skin again, and distract them.'

Uncas folded his arms, and leaned against the wall of the hut.

'Uncas will stay', said the Mohican. 'He will fight with his father's brother, and die with the friend of the Mohicans.'

'I'm glad', said Hawkeye. 'Let's try another plan. Put on the bear skin. I'm sure you can play the part of a bear.'

Hawkeye turned to Gamut. 'Take my hunting shirt and my cap', he said, 'and give me your blanket and your hat. Also your book, your glasses, and the whistle too, if you don't mind. I'll give everything back to you if we ever meet again. If you agree to stay here, you must sit here in the shadows and pretend to be Uncas. You can make a run for it², or you can wait here.'

'I will stay here', said Gamut.

Hawkeye shook Gamut's hand. Then he left the lodge accompanied by Uncas, dressed in the bear skin. In front of the Hurons, Hawkeye imitated Gamut's appearance and movements. He sang a hymn and waved his arm in time with his singing, just as Gamut did. The two men moved forward slowly, acting as if everything was normal.

They were close to the woods when they heard a loud cry from the lodge. Uncas stood upright and shook off his furry covering. Behind them, shouting filled the air. Hawkeye and Uncas continued walking and soon they found themselves safe in the darkness of the forest.

ESCAPE

★ Explain in your own words how:
   ☐ Alice and Heyward escaped.
   ☐ Uncas and Hawkeye escaped.
★ What do you think happens to Gamut?

---

1 glittering ['glɪtərɪŋ] (a.) 閃閃發光的
2 make a run for it 逃之夭夭

CHAPTER 15

The Indians had waited outside the lodge. They did not want the medicine man to breathe on them, but they were impatient[1]. They wanted to see what was happening inside. They moved cautiously[2] towards the entrance, with their hearts beating fast, and they looked through a hole in the door. Inside they could see Uncas sitting by the fire. They watched him for several minutes but when he turned his head, they realized it was Gamut. They gave a loud cry, rushed into the lodge and grabbed him.

Gamut believed that his final hour had come. The Indians wanted vengeance[3]. He no longer had his book and his whistle, but he could still sing something from memory. He prepared for his arrival in the next world by singing a funeral[4] hymn. This helped to remind the Indians that he was completely mad and they left him alone.

Soon the whole village knew that their prisoner had escaped. Over two hundred men waited outside the lodge for the command from their chiefs to chase and catch Uncas. Just one important person was missing.

'Where is Magua?' said one of the chiefs.

'Go to his hut', said another. 'Bring him here quickly. We need him.'

The oldest and most respected chiefs met and discussed the situation. The father of the sick woman arrived and told the chiefs about the visit of the doctor, and about the strange bear that followed them to the cave. The council members sent ten of their wisest chiefs to investigate[5].

In the dark and silent cave, the men found the sick woman lying in her bed.

'It's not possible', said one of the chiefs. 'We saw the medicine man carry her into the woods.'

The woman's father approached the side of the bed. He bent over his daughter's face and looked at it carefully. Then suddenly, in a voice full of grief[6], he cried, 'The Great Spirit is angry with his children. My daughter is dead!'

One of the chiefs started to speak. A noise interrupted him. A dark object rolled into the centre of the cave from the next room.

'Magua!' exclaimed the warriors when they saw the angry snarling[7] face of the Huron chief.

He was tied up from hand to foot. When he was released, he got up, his face black with rage[8].

'Let the Mohican die!' shouted Magua, in a voice like thunder.

The room was silent. Then one of the chiefs said, 'The Mohican runs fast, but our young warriors will catch him.'

'He escaped?' said Magua. 'You let him escape?'

'It was not our fault', said the chief. 'An evil spirit was among us and it blinded us'.

'An evil spirit!' said Magua scornfully. 'It is the same spirit that killed so many Hurons, that took the scalps of my warriors and that tied me up and left me in this cave!'

'Who does my friend speak of?'

'I speak of one who has pale skin, but who has the heart and craftiness[9] of a Huron', said Magua. 'I am speaking of Hawkeye!'

---

1 impatient [ɪmˋpeʃənt] (a.) 無耐心的
2 cautiously [ˋkɔʃəslɪ] (adv.) 謹慎地
3 vengeance [ˋvɛndʒəns] (n.) 報仇
4 funeral [ˋfjunərəl] (a.) 喪葬的
5 investigate [ɪnˋvɛstəˌget] (v.) 調查
6 grief [grif] (n.) 悲慟
7 snarling [ˋsnɑrlɪŋ] (a.) 咆哮的
8 rage [redʒ] (n.) 憤怒
9 craftiness [ˋkræftɪnəs] (n.) 詭詐；狡猾

When the new day dawned, twenty warriors waited outside Magua's hut. The council members had placed Magua in charge[1]. Now his men were ready. He led them silently past a winding[2] stream and then along the side of a small lake. As they passed, the head of a large beaver appeared from behind some rocks. The animal seemed to watch their movements with interest. The warriors entered the forest. Then the beaver came out from the rocks, took off its mask of fur and revealed the serious face of Chingachgook the Mohican.

1 place sb in charge 讓某人擔任負責人
2 winding [ˋwaɪdɪŋ] (a.) 彎曲的；曲折的

Magua arrived later that day at the village of the Delawares. 'The wise Huron is welcome', said one of the Delaware chiefs. 'I hope my prisoner is not causing problems', said Magua.

'She is welcome', said the Delaware chief.

'If she is giving my brother trouble, then I will send her to my camp', said Magua.

'No, she is welcome,' repeated the chief.

'I think there are strange moccasins in the woods,' said Magua looking around him. 'And here in your village perhaps?'

'Who does my brother speak of?' said the chief.

'Of our mortal enemy, Hawkeye, The Long Rifle', said Magua.

The chief spoke quietly to his companions. More warriors and important chiefs arrived and joined the group. All of them were surprised and concerned[1] when they heard Magua's news. The Delaware council decided to call a meeting of the whole tribe.

Early the next morning a thousand warriors waited outside the lodge to hear the words of their chiefs. Three men appeared in front of the multitude[2]. All three were very old but one of them, who leaned on his companions for support, was more than a hundred years old. He shuffled[3] slowly and painfully across the ground. His dark and wrinkled[4] face contrasted with the color of his long white hair. The warriors whispered the name of 'Tamenund'. They knew that Tamenund was wise and just[5], and that he had the gift of communicating with the Great Spirit.

The huge crowd made a circle around the old man and the other council members. There was silence. Then a group of warriors brought in the prisoners.

WISDOM

★ What does it mean to be wise?
★ Write a definition and compare with a partner.
★ Who do you consider to be wise?

CHAPTER 16

Cora stood with her arms around Alice. She showed no fear of the fierce-looking Indians who surrounded her. Next to her stood Heyward. Behind him was Hawkeye. Uncas was not with them. One of Tamenund's old chiefs asked in English, 'Which prisoner is The Long Rifle?'

No one answered. Heyward saw Magua staring at Cora. She looked back at him calmly. Magua took hold of Alice's arm and started to lead her away. Cora ran to Tamenund and knelt at his feet.

---

1 concerned [kən'sɜˈnd] (a.) 擔心的
2 multitude ['mʌltə,tjud] (n.) 群眾
3 shuffle ['ʃʌfl] (v.) 拖著腳走
4 wrinkled ['rɪŋkld] (a.) 有皺紋的
5 just [dʒʌst] (a.) 公正的

In a loud voice she said, 'Just and noble Delaware, we depend on your wisdom for mercy! You have lived so long and you have seen the evil of the world. Do not believe this man Magua. He poisons[1] your ears with lies. He is thirsty for blood.'

Everyone looked at Tamenund and waited. The old man stood up and spoke.

'Who are you?' he said.

'I come from a race of people that you hate', said Cora, 'but I have never harmed your people and I am here to ask for your help. Tell me, is Tamenund a father?'

The old man smiled. He looked around him at the great crowd and answered: 'Yes, I am the father of a nation.'

Cora continued. 'I ask nothing for myself, but the young woman over there is the daughter of an old man whose life is nearly over. Many people love her and she is much too good and too precious to become the victim of that evil man. Before you let the Huron leave with this woman, call the other man who was with us. He is one of your own people. Please hear him speak.'

'He is a redskin who works for the enemy', said one of the chiefs to Tamenund. 'We are keeping him so that we can torture him.'

'Bring him here', said Tamenund.

A few minutes later Uncas was standing in the middle of the circle.

'What language does the prisoner speak?' asked Tamenund.

'Like his fathers', said Uncas, 'the language of the Delawares.'

'Who are you?' asked Tamenund.

---

1 poison [ˈpɔɪzn̩] (v.) 毒害

 'I am Uncas, the son of Chingachgook.' Uncas stood proudly in front of the crowd as he spoke these words.

Now in the light Tamenund could see that on his chest Uncas had a tattoo of a small blue tortoise.

'My race', said Uncas, 'is the grandfather of a nation. I am a son of the great Unamis the Turtle.'

The old man opened his eyes wide. 'Tamenund's time is over!' he exclaimed. 'I thank the Great Spirit. At last someone is here to fill my place at the council-fire. We have found Uncas, the son of Chingachgook. Now the eyes of a dying eagle can look at the rising sun.'

CHAPTER 17

 Uncas stood proudly next to Tamenund, where the whole crowd could see him.

'It is true', he told them. 'The blood of the turtle has been in many chiefs, but all of them are dead now, except for Chingachgook and his son.'

Uncas looked into the crowd and saw Hawkeye with his hands tied. Immediately he went to his friend and cut his bonds. Then he led Hawkeye to Tamenund.

'Father', he said, 'this man with the pale face is a just man and he is the friend of the Delawares.'

Tamenund nodded. 'And what about the woman that the Huron brought into my village?' he asked.

'She is mine,' cried Magua, shaking his hand in triumph at Uncas.

Uncas did not speak.

'My son is silent,' said Tamenund.

'Mohican, you know that she is mine', said Magua.

'It is true,' said Uncas sadly, 'but do not make her go with him.'

'The wigwam of Magua is empty', said the Huron. 'He needs a wife and children of his own.'

Tamenund turned to Cora. 'Girl, what do you want? A great warrior is taking you as his wife. Go with him and your race will not end. You will have children and grandchildren'.

'I would prefer to die than suffer such degradation[1]', said Cora.

'Huron,' said Tamenund, 'this woman's mind is in the tents of her fathers. An unwilling[2] wife makes an unhappy wigwam.'

'Let Tamenund agree', said Magua.

---

1 degradation [ˌdɛɡrəˈdeʃən] (n.) 恥辱
2 unwilling [ʌnˈwɪlɪŋ] (a.) 不情願的

LOVE

★ Magua wants Cora as his wife, but she doesn't want to live with Magua. What are the most important things for you in a successful relationship? Write three things.

'Go, but take with you only what you brought here', said Tamenund. 'The Great Spirit does not allow us to be unjust.'

Magua came forward and grabbed Cora by the arm.

'Wait! Wait!' said Heyward. 'Huron, have mercy! The white woman's ransom[1] will make you richer than any of your people.'

'Magua is a redskin. He does not need the money of the pale faces.'

The Huron pushed Cora forward.

'There is no need for violence', said Cora. 'I will come in a moment.'

Alice had fainted and was lying in Heyward's arms. Cora bent over her and kissed her. Then she said to Magua, 'Now I am ready to go.'

She followed Magua and his warriors through the crowd.

'The Delawares cannot stop you, Magua', cried Heyward, 'but I can.'

'No', said Hawkeye, 'Do not follow him. He will lead you to your death.'

'Huron', shouted Uncas, 'Look at the sun. When the sun is high above the trees, we will follow you.'

'Delawares, you are dogs, rabbits and thieves. I spit[2] on you', Magua replied, and before he and Cora entered the forest, he gave Heyward and Uncas one last scornful look.

1 ransom [ˈrænsəm] (n.) 贖金
2 spit [spɪt] (v.) 吐口水 (以表示輕蔑)

CHAPTER 18

When the sun was high, Uncas threw his tomahawk into a tree and gave a loud battle cry. The young warriors were armed and painted and ready for battle. Uncas prepared to lead them in search of their enemy.

Heyward left Alice in the care of the Delaware women and then went to join Hawkeye. Uncas gave Hawkeye the command of twenty warriors. The Mohican met with his chiefs and gave them his orders. When Uncas left the village more than two hundred men marched by his side.

In the forest the Indians stopped to discuss their plan. Just then a man appeared in the distance.

'He must be one of Magua's warriors', said Uncas.

'His time has come,' said Hawkeye, raising his rifle and taking aim. But, after a few moments, he put down his rifle.

'I was sure he was a Huron', said Hawkeye. 'I was wrong!'

The man who came nervously towards the Delawares was Gamut. He looked happier when he saw the familiar faces of Uncas and Hawkeye.

'Have you seen the Hurons?' asked Hawkeye.

'They're everywhere', said Gamut. 'They're hiding in the forest.'

'What about Magua?' said Uncas.

'He's with them', said Gamut. 'Cora was with him and he has left her in a cave.'

'I will follow the stream with my warriors', said Hawkeye, 'and I will meet Chingachgook and Munro. Then I will signal to you, Uncas, and you must move forward. When the Hurons are in the range[1] of our rifles, we will shoot. After that, we will rescue Cora from the cave.'

The men discussed the plan in greater detail. When everything was agreed, Hawkeye led his men toward the stream. He stopped there and waited until his warriors were close by. He spoke to them in Delaware.

'Men, we will hide here until we smell the Hurons', he said. He turned to Gamut. 'Remember', he said, 'No singing. When I give the signal, only our rifles will sing.'

Gamut nodded, and Hawkeye gave a sign to his men to proceed[2].

After they had gone just a few steps, shots rang out. One of the Delawares fell dead.

'Take cover', shouted Hawkeye.

The Delawares moved forward cautiously and fired their rifles. Heyward did the same. The Hurons hid behind the trees and fired back. The Hurons were attacking on all sides, but Hawkeye realized that it would be more dangerous to retreat[3] than to advance. It seemed as though the tribe was surrounding them. Then they heard the yells of Uncas and his men.

---

1 in the range 在射程內
2 proceed [prə'sid] (v.) 繼續前進
3 retreat [rɪ'trit] (v.) 撤退

'Move forward', shouted Hawkeye.

The Delawares ran forward and attacked the Hurons. They fought hand to hand. The Hurons retreated until they reached a thick wooded area. They hid there in the bushes. Suddenly, from behind the Hurons there came rifle fire. Hawkeye and the others heard the fierce yell of a war cry.

'Chingachgook!' said Hawkeye. 'Now the Hurons are surrounded.'

The Huron warriors had nowhere to hide. They ran in every direction, trying to avoid the bullets and the tomahawks of the Delawares. Some escaped but many died.

'Be prepared', said Hawkeye. 'More Hurons are coming.'

Heyward looked at Chingachgook. He was sitting calmly on a rock.

'The Delawares must attack!' said Heyward.

'Not yet', said Hawkeye. 'Chingachgook will wait for the right moment.'

At that moment Chingachgook shouted the war cry and the Delawares fired their rifles. A dozen Hurons fell dead. From the forest came another war cry. The Hurons were confused. A hundred Delaware warriors came out of the forest. Leading them was Uncas. The Hurons ran, followed by the Delawares. One small group of Hurons separated from the others and climbed slowly up a hill. In the middle of them was Magua. It was easy to recognize him from his proud and fierce appearance.

As soon as he saw his enemy, Uncas shouted and six or seven warriors came to join him. Magua smiled when he saw Uncas approach. The Huron and his men outnumbered[1] Uncas and his Delawares. Magua aimed his rifle, but before he could fire, Hawkeye and his men joined the attack. Magua turned and quickly retreated up the hill.

Uncas, Hawkeye and Munro fought a fierce battle with Magua's Hurons. Soon the ground was covered with the dead warriors. Only two warriors escaped with Magua. They ran from the scene of the battle. Uncas ran up the hill to find Magua. Hawkeye, Heyward and Gamut followed. Magua ran through thick bushes and then into a cave in the side of the mountain.

'Now we have him', shouted Hawkeye.

But when the men entered the cave, the Hurons were disappearing into a long passage. They saw something else, a white dress.

'It's Cora', shouted Heyward.

The two Huron warriors were dragging her with them through the cave. Magua was leading them.

Uncas shook his tomahawk at Magua. 'Wait, you dogs', he shouted.

Cora stopped at the edge of the rocks. There was a sheer[2] drop[3] beneath her.

'I will go no further', she cried. 'Kill me if you want to, Huron. I will go no further.'

'Woman', said Magua, 'choose the wigwam or Magua's knife!'

Magua raised his arm. The blade of his knife glittered in the light. Magua hesitated, and then he lowered his arm. He looked at Cora as though he was not sure what to do. But, just then there was a loud shout from above them. Uncas appeared. He jumped down onto the rocks. Magua stepped back in surprise.

At that moment one of Magua's warriors took hold of Cora and stabbed his own knife into her heart. Cora fell down dead. Magua in a rage of anger and shock tried to attack the other Huron, but Uncas was in his way. Magua raised his knife, screamed and stabbed Uncas in the back. Uncas stood up and struck[4] Cora's murderer. The Indian fell to the ground.

Then Uncas turned to look at Magua. Magua seized[5] Uncas's arm and then thrust[6] his knife into the Mohican's heart several times. Uncas stared at Magua scornfully[7]. He slipped out of Magua's hands and fell dead at his feet.

THE BATTLE

★ What happens during the battle for Cora?
★ With a partner write what happens step by step.
★ Think about what happens to the following people:
　☐Cora　☐Hawkeye　☐Heyward　☐Magua　☐Uncas

---

1 outnumber [autˋnʌmbɚ] (v.) 數目勝過
2 sheer [ʃɪr] (a.) 陡峭的
3 drop [drɑp] (n.) 瀑布
4 strike [straɪk] (v.) 攻擊

5 seize [siz] (v.) 抓住
6 thrust [θrʌst] (v.) 刺
7 scornfully [ˋskɔrnfəlɪ] (adv.) 輕蔑地

Heyward watched the scene in horror from the rocks above. 'Have mercy!', he cried.

Magua responded by waving his bloody knife at Heyward and giving a triumphant war cry. Everyone who was fighting in the valley a thousand feet below heard him. Hawkeye ran along the edge of the rocks, but all he found were the bodies of the dead.

'Catch him', shouted Hawkeye.

Magua leapt over a gap[1] in the rocks. Neither Hawkeye nor Gamut could reach him.

'If he jumps to the next rock, he'll get away', said Gamut.

Magua stood on a precipice[2], high on the mountainside. He was just one jump away from safety. He paused and shook his fist[3] at Hawkeye.

'The pale faces are dogs!' he shouted. 'The Delawares are cowards. Magua leaves them on the rocks for the crows!'

He laughed and then he jumped, but he miscalculated[4]. He did not jump far enough. He reached out desperately to grab a bush and save himself. He started to pull himself up.

Hawkeye aimed his rifle and fired. Magua's arms relaxed. His body became loose[5]. He turned to look at Hawkeye. His expression was angry and defiant[6]. He let go of the bush and he fell, head first, down the side of the mountain, down and down into the valley.

---

1 gap [gæp] (n.) 峽谷；山口
2 precipice [ˈprɛsəpɪs] (n.) 斷崖
3 fist [fɪst] (n.) 拳頭
4 miscalculate [mɪsˈkælkjəˌlet] (v.) 算錯；誤估
5 loose [lus] (a.) 鬆掉了的

6 defiant [dɪˈfaɪənt] (a.) 公然反抗的
7 mourner [ˈmornɚ] (n.) 送葬者
8 sorrowfully [ˈsɑrəfəlɪ] (adv.) 悲傷地
9 heartbroken [ˈhɑrtˌbrokən] (a.) 極為傷心的
10 wagon [ˈwægən] (n.) 運貨馬車

CHAPTER 19

 The following day, the Delawares were a nation of mourners[7]. Officers from the British and the French armies attended the funeral ceremony. Six Delaware girls, with long, dark hair threw herbs and forest flowers over Cora's body. Munro sat in tears at her feet. Gamut stood next to him with his head bowed.

The tribe had placed the body of Uncas on a throne. He sat there dressed in rich robes and glittering ornaments, with bright feathers above his head. Chingachgook sat without moving in front of his son's body, staring at his face. Hawkeye stood close by, leaning on his rifle. Resting on the arms of two of his chiefs, Tamenund also watched and listened. He looked down sorrowfully[8] on the crowd.

A warrior began to speak. 'Why have you left us?' he said to the dead Uncas. 'Your glory was brighter than the midday sun. You have gone, young warrior, but a hundred Delawares are clearing your path to the world of the spirits.'

The Delaware women carried Cora's body to a place of burial. Gamut read from his bible over the grave.

Then Munro spoke. 'Cora, my child, your father is heartbroken[9] and offers you his prayers.' Then, looking at Heyward and Gamut, he said, 'Come, gentlemen, our duty here is complete. Now let us leave.'

Alice, still weeping, climbed into the wagon[10] that they had prepared for her. The men shook hands with Hawkeye, mounted their horses and rode into the forest with the army officers following them.

When Hawkeye returned to Chingachgook's side, the Indians were placing Uncas in his resting place. His body faced the rising sun. Next to him were weapons of war and hunting. He was ready for his final journey. The Delaware warriors closed the grave so that wild animals could not enter it.

Chingachgook spoke. 'Why do my brothers mourn? Why do my daughters cry? A young man has gone to the happy hunting-grounds. A chief has completed his time with honor. He was good. He was brave. He did his duty. The Great Spirit needed such a warrior and has called Uncas to join him.'

Chingachgook looked around him. 'My race has gone from the shores of the salt lake and from the hills of the Delawares', he said. 'I am alone.'

'No, no,' cried Hawkeye. 'Our color may be different, but God has sent us to travel on the same path. You are not alone.'

Chingachgook took Hawkeye's hand warmly and the two men bowed their heads together. Their tears fell to the ground and watered the grave of Uncas like drops of falling rain.

Tamenund spoke. 'It is enough,' he said. 'My day has been too long. And yet, before my night has come, I have lived to see the last warrior of the wise race of the Mohicans.'

AFTER READING

Ⓐ Personal Response

1 Before you finished reading, did you guess how the story would end? Tell the class.

2 Now that you have read the story, can you explain why it is called *The Last of the Mohicans*?

3 Work with a partner. Imagine you are making a film of *The Last of the Mohicans*. Which parts of the book would you change or rewrite? Would you add any new characters? Would you remove or change any of the existing characters?

4 Did you like the ending of the story? Why? Why not? Discuss this with your partner. Together write a different ending for the story. Tell your new ending to the rest of the class.

5 Imagine you are living in this period of history. Which would you rather be, a native American Indian, a soldier from Europe, or a frontiersman like Hawkeye?

6 What, in your opinion, is the most important part of the story? What is the most exciting part? Find out what your partner thinks. Is there any part of the story that you both found boring? Why didn't you like that part of the story?

❶ Comprehension

🗣 **7** Work with a partner. One of you read the A Questions
and one of you read the B Questions. Check that you
know the answers to your own questions. Then, ask your
partner to answer your questions.

> **A Questions**
>
> * Who was the commander of Fort William Henry?
> * What nationality was Montcalm?
> * What tribe did Magua belong to?
> * How did Heyward and his party get lost?
> * How did the group travel to Hawkeye's secret hiding place?
> * Who was injured when the Hurons attacked for the first time?

> **B Questions**
>
> * Which Indian language did Hawkeye and the Mohicans speak?
> * What does the name Chingachgook mean?
> * Who was 'The Long Rifle'?
> * Where was Cora's mother from?
> * Which sister does Magua want to take as his wife?
> * Which two characters are killed at the end of the story?

🗣 **8** Work with your partner. Write four more questions
based on the story. Find another pair and ask them your
questions.

9 Can you match these sentences from the story with their meanings?

> 1 How many soldiers have we got?
> 2 I am old, but you are young.
> 3 He thought he was going to die.
> 4 Our prisoner escaped.
> 5 Can I marry your daughter?

_____ a Gamut believed his final hour had come.

_____ b Do you know the strength of our army?

_____ c Will you allow me the honor of being your son?

_____ d The eyes of a dying eagle can look at the rising sun.

_____ e The Mohican runs fast, but our young warriors will catch him.

10 Put the events from the story in the correct order.

__1__ a Cora, Alice and Heyward left Fort Edward to travel to Fort William Henry.

_____ b Magua killed Uncas.

_____ c The British surrendered the fort to Montcalm.

_____ d Hawkeye took Cora and Alice back to their father at Fort William Henry.

_____ e Hawkeye helped to rescue Alice by pretending to be a bear.

_____ f The Delawares buried Uncas and Cora side by side.

_____ g Magua's Indians attacked the people who were leaving the fort.

_____ h Hawkeye and the Mohicans helped Munro and Heyward to find the women.

_____ i Tamenund declared Uncas to be the chief of the tribe.

_____ j Magua tried to escape but Hawkeye shot him.

_____ k A Huron stabbed Cora in the heart.

_____ l Heyward's party was betrayed by Magua the Indian guide.

❻ Characters

11 Who is your favorite character? Write notes about him/her.

Name

Nationality/Tribe

Appearance

Skills/Abilities

12 Read the sentences below. Who do they describe – Alice or Cora?

_____ ⓐ She has long golden hair.
_____ ⓑ She enjoys singing.
_____ ⓒ She is a calm and quiet person.
_____ ⓓ She is easily frightened.
_____ ⓔ She thinks of other people before herself.
_____ ⓕ She cries a lot.
_____ ⓖ She is very wise.

13 What do you think about the author's female characters Alice and Cora? Which would you choose as your friend, and why? Tell the class.

14 Write the names of the characters beside the sentences.

_____ a) He had a tattoo of a small blue tortoise on his chest.

_____ b) He pretended to be Uncas.

_____ c) He pretended to be a doctor.

_____ d) He carried a tomahawk and a knife, and wore no ornaments except for an eagle's feather.

_____ e) He met his wife in the West Indies.

_____ f) He wore Indian moccasins and buckskin trousers.

_____ g) He pretended he didn't know any English.

_____ h) He sent no reinforcements to Fort William Henry.

_____ i) He was courteous and welcoming.

15 Imagine you are a journalist. What questions would you ask Heyward? Ask and answer with a partner.

16 Describe the relationship between the following characters. What have they got in common? How are they different? What is the link between them?

a) Hawkeye and Chingachgook

b) Cora and Alice

c) Alice and Heyward

d) Cora and Magua

e) Munro and Montcalm

D Plot and Theme

17 What kind of novel is *The Last of the Mohicans*? Tick (✓) below.

_____ a An historical novel
_____ b A romantic novel
_____ c A fantasy novel
_____ d An adventure novel

18 Tell the class and give reasons for your answer.

19 Which of the following themes is present in *The Last of the Mohicans*. Put a tick (✓) for yes and a cross (×) for no.

_____ a Love between people of different races.
_____ b Man's love of nature.
_____ c The power of superstition.
_____ d The importance of brotherhood between people of different races.
_____ e The struggle for power.
_____ f The role of religion.
_____ g The importance of racial tolerance.

20 Can you think of any other themes that are present in the novel?

21 In your opinion, what ideas or messages does the author want to convey to his readers? Choose below and give examples from the text to support your answer.

_____ a Nature is difficult and hostile.
_____ b The family is important to the structure of society.
_____ c Native Americans are simple, uneducated people.
_____ d Romances between people of different races end in tragedy.
_____ e Human beings can determine their own fate.
_____ f It is easy to fool uneducated people.
_____ g Good always triumphs over evil.
_____ h We should never trust anyone.

22 Some of the events in *The Last of the Mohicans* have a symbolic meaning. Can you match the people or events with the descriptions.

1 The mixture of Indian culture and European culture.
2 The representative of two cultures – black and white.
3 The end of Indian culture.
4 Evil.

_____ a Hawkeye
_____ b Magua
_____ c The death of Uncas
_____ d Cora

TEST

1 Match the first parts of these sentences with their correct endings.

> 1 he won't go very far.
> 2 we will have help in less than two hours.
> 3 it will send him to his grave.
> 4 he'll get away.
> 5 he will lead us straight into an ambush.
> 6 everyone will die.

_____ a If Montcalm attacks Fort William Henry_____
_____ b If Magua is wounded _____
_____ c If we follow Magua _____
_____ d If my old father loses both his daughters _____
_____ e If they reach General Webb _____
_____ f If Magua jumps to the next rock _____

2 Use the prompts below to write questions in the Present Perfect.

Example: Hawkeye/ever/fire a rifle?
↳ Has Hawkeye ever fired a rifle?

a Gamut/ever/use a compass?
b Cora and Alice/ever/ride a horse?
c Heyward/ever/learn a foreign language?
d Cora/ever/be married?
e Chingachgook/ever/visit the graves of his fathers?
f Magua and Montcalm/ever/meet?

🔊 3 Work with a partner to ask and answer the questions above.

Example: Has Hawkeye ever fired a rifle?
↳ Yes, he has.

4 Complete the questions with **How long, How old** or **How many**. Then answer the questions correctly.

a _____ _____ did it take Magua to run to Fort Edward from Fort William Henry?

b _____ _____ men did Montcalm have?

c _____ _____ was Munro married to Cora's mother?

d _____ _____ languages did Heyward speak?

e _____ _____ was Alice?

f _____ _____ had the war between the French and the English lasted?

g _____ _____ was Tamenund?

5 Choose **could / was able to / managed to**.

a Uncas was able to / couldn't / managed to swim down the river to safety.

b Heyward could / wasn't able to / managed to help Alice because his hands were tied together.

c Cora was able to / could / didn't manage to leave her glove behind as a clue.

d Cora could / managed to / wasn't able to stay calm when she spoke to Magua.

e The bullets from the Indian's rifles could not / were not able to / didn't manage to reach them.

f The old squaw managed to / could / wasn't able to frighten the Huron warrior.

TRANSLATION

作者簡介　詹姆士‧庫柏於 1789 年出生於美國新澤西州的柏靈頓。他在家中十二名兄弟姊妹中排行十一，他的父親威廉和母親伊麗莎白是貴格會的教徒。他父親是一位大地主，在紐約州開創了「庫柏鎮」。他在成長過程中，很喜歡探索住家附近的田野森林。

他在十七歲時加入海軍，接下來五年的歲月都在航海中度過。二十歲時，他繼承家產，並在兩年後結婚。他曾有一段時間以農為業。他生活無虞，有時間從事閱讀之類的活動。他研究美國歷史和北美的生活。

有一次，在寫完一篇小說後，他跟妻子說，他要寫出更好的東西一點也不難。妻子鼓勵他嘗試，他開始爬格子，於 1820 年出版了第一本小說。他持續創作，出版了四十餘本書籍，其中包括社會科學和政治評論。

他最有名的著作是五本「皮裏腿故事」系列，描寫美國拓荒者的故事，《最後的摩希根人》（1826 年出版）即是當中的一本。這系列故事中的英雄人物叫做 Natty Bumppo，他又名「鷹眼」或「皮裏腿」。

1826 到 1833 年期間，庫柏遊歷了歐洲，他住過倫敦、巴黎和義大利的索倫托。他透過著作，主要要向讀者傳達社會責任、民主政治、美國歷史和美國的文化傳統。

1851 年，庫柏於家鄉庫柏鎮辭世。

本書簡介　《最後的摩希根人》的場景設在 1757 年的夏天，時值北美印地安戰爭時期，英國和法國為爭奪紐約州西部而開戰。

威廉亨利堡是英國的前哨基地，由穆羅上校所負責，後來遭到法國指揮官孟康和同盟的印地安人攻擊，這些印地安人來自胡龍族和達拉威部落。穆羅上校的兩個女兒——愛麗絲和蔻若——前來找他們的父親，卻在途中被胡龍族的馬瓜所挾持，因為馬瓜想向宿敵穆羅上校報一箭之仇。

一位叫做鷹眼的早期移民後代，他身懷絕技，和欽加哥、安卡斯兩位摩希根人營救了兩位姊妹。他們歷經了多次危險的交戰，千鈞一髮，最後在奮戰中以悲劇收場。

《最後的摩希根人》是一本虛構小說，但故事中有些橋段以真實的歷史事件為背景，例如 1757 年八月威廉亨利堡的投降事件。投降之後，殖民者棄堡離開，卻遭到法國的印地安同盟者攻擊，最後有 180 個人左右在事件中喪生。

CHAPTER 1

P.13

馬瓜從威廉亨利堡出發已經走了兩個鐘頭，這位印地安戰士一路上急急奔跑，穿過濃密的樹林，通過陰蔽的小路，直奔愛德華堡。穆羅上校要他帶一個緊急的情報，給愛德華堡的英國指揮官魏伯將軍。

「法國指揮官孟康正朝著威廉亨利堡推進過來了。」馬瓜說。

馬瓜帶來的情報，引起堡內居民和外圍駐紮的英國士兵一片慌張。

「孟康麾軍善戰，旗下有很多士兵和印地安戰士。他要是攻打威廉亨利堡，一定會殺個寸草不留，穆羅上校也會沒命，孟康的印地安戰士會取下英國士兵的頭顱。穆羅上校需要更多的兵力和物資。」

愛德華堡的居民人人惶恐不安。

魏伯將軍聽著馬瓜的報告，不發一語。法國和英國正打得腥風血雨，為了爭奪這個蠻荒異域，雙方已經交戰三年了。

P.14

「孟康有多少人馬？」魏伯將軍問。

「他們的人馬『多如樹葉』，你一定要派兵過去支援。」馬瓜回答。

魏伯將軍仍保持沉著。

「你很有膽量，謝謝你送情報來。我有事時會再叫你。」魏伯將軍說。

翌日，魏伯將軍派了一千五百名士兵動身前往威廉亨利堡，這段路要花上一整天的行程。

旅程

- 你走過最長的旅程有多遠？
- 你當時的交通工具是什麼？搭車、搭飛機，還是坐公車？
- 你為了這段旅程做了哪些準備？

在魏伯將軍的營外，僕人正在準備上路要用的馬匹。好奇的居民圍觀過來，其中有一個叫做大衛‧加慕的人，他長得瘦瘦高高、手長腳長。

「這不是普通的馬，這是專門要給重要人物坐的馬，好像是要給兩位女士和一位軍官坐的。」加慕說罷，人群對他露出佩服的眼光。

「我是傳教士，也兼做馬匹買賣，所以這種事我熟啦。」加慕解釋道。他轉身看看那些正在聽他講話的人群，留意到印地安人馬瓜一臉驚慌的神色。馬瓜的臉畫著戰紋，配戴著戰斧和刀子。他們兩個人對望了一下。

這時，有一位年輕的軍官和兩位女士從屋子裡走出來。兩位女士都帶著面紗帽子，遮住了臉。當軍官扶起年紀較小的女孩坐上馬匹時，風吹開了她的面紗。

P.15

加慕看到她有一雙明亮的藍色眼眸，和一頭金色的長髮。另外一位女子也一樣姿色動人，留著一頭烏黑的秀髮，年紀大個四、五歲左右。他們三個人騎上馬匹，向魏伯將軍告

別，然後帶著一行僕人離開軍營。

馬瓜跟在他們後面跑。他跑過年少女孩的馬匹，來到馬匹前方的路。較年長的女子，帶著既欽佩又同情的眼光看著這個印地安人。當他溜過年少女孩的旁邊時，女孩嚇了一大跳，發出了叫聲。

「別怕，愛麗絲。這個印地安人是陸軍的探子，他叫馬瓜，他會帶我們走湖邊的路，我們會比軍隊提早抵達威廉亨利堡。」軍官説。

「何歐，你相信這個人？」愛麗絲問。

「我相信啊，他以前投奔過毛火族，曾經是您父親穆羅上校的敵人，不過這都是很久以前的事了。他現在是我們這邊的人。」軍官説。

P.16

「馬瓜會説英語嗎？你能叫他説説看嗎？」愛麗絲問。

何歐笑了笑，説：「他都裝成不懂英語的樣子，除非必要，不然他是不會開口説英語的。」

這時，印地安人停下腳步，用手指指著樹叢裡一條只容一匹馬勉強通過的蔭暗小路。

「我們是不是應該跟著軍隊走，我覺得跟馬瓜不是很可靠。」愛麗絲説。

「難道就因為他的舉止和我們不一樣、皮膚比較黑，就不信任他？」黑髮女孩説。

愛麗絲沒有回應姊姊的話，她騎著馬，跟在馬瓜後面進入樹叢，沿著群樹之間的濃蔭小路走下去。

偏見

- 愛麗絲不信任馬瓜，她這種態度對馬瓜來説公平嗎？
- 你初次和人見面時，你會如何來評價對方？是透過對方的穿著、講話方式、行為方式還是膚色來判斷？

他們一行人繼續通過樹林。

「現在那些僕人一定要走別條路，我們單獨走，這樣孟康手下的印地安人就更不容易發現我們的足跡。」馬瓜説。

何歐要僕人走士兵走的路，然後自己和兩位姊妹按原路走，由馬瓜跑在前面帶路。

這時，突然傳來一陣馬蹄聲。他們屏住呼吸，待在樹叢裡想知道是什麼人跟在他們後面。

P.17

「是誰？」何歐問。

「我叫大衛·加慕，我是一位傳教士，在擔任唱聖歌。」男子説道。

愛麗絲聽到他這麼一説，心寬多了。

「何歐，就讓他跟我們一起走吧，我在愛德華堡看過他。加慕先生可以騎在我旁邊，我可以和他一起唱歌。」愛麗絲説。

加慕於是開口唱起歌來，但馬瓜要何歐立刻制止他。

「加慕先生，很抱歉，你的歌聲很動人，但現在這種場合，請一路上保持安

靜。」何歐説。

「何歐，你為什麼老是這麼掃興？我們現在玩得很開心。」愛麗絲説。

「等我們到了目地的，會有很多機會唱歌。沒有人知道我們的方位，我們要確保我們的行蹤不會被發現。」何歐説。

這四個人騎著馬穿過樹林，他們沒有發現有個臉上刺青的印地安人正躲在樹叢裡盯著他們。

CHAPTER 2

P.18

這是一個七月的黃昏，在一條小溪旁，坐著一個印地安人和一個白人，他們在那裡歇息，小聲講著話。這裡一片寧靜，只有鳥鳴聲和遠處的瀑布聲。印地安人配帶著戰斧和刀子，頭上插著一根老鷹的羽毛，沒有別的裝飾品。他的頭剃得很光潔，只留著一束短髮，大腿上橫擱著一把來福槍。他已經不是小伙子的年紀，但看起來很結實，精力旺盛。

旁邊的白人一身肌肉，皮膚曬得黑黑的，長得很老實的樣子。他穿著一件鑲有黃色流蘇的綠色襯衫，頭上戴著一頂獸皮帽子，穿著印地安式的鹿皮鞋和褲子。他的腰帶上佩戴著刀子、彈藥袋和牛角，身旁立著一支靠在樹幹上的長步槍。他講印地安話，他一邊説話，一邊四面觀察，留意附近是否藏有敵人。

「鷹眼，你和我是不一樣的。你的祖先從太陽落下的地方過來，我的祖先從太陽升起的紅色天空那邊過來。」印地安人説。

欽加哥説：「我們從遙遠的野牛草原來到這大河邊，和雅力圭人開戰，血洗了這塊地方。我們來到了鹽湖邊，馬郭人尾隨我們，我們把他們趕進樹林裡。很久很久之後，來了第一批白人。白人坐著大船，橫越大海而來。當時我們偃旗息鼓，部落團結，生活太平。湖泊給我們魚，森林給我們鹿，天空給我們鳥。」

P.20

「我相信你的祖先很有智慧，都是英勇的戰士。」鷹眼説。

「我的身上流著酋長的血液，我的部落是許多部落的祖先。白人來到這裡，給我們的人『火水』（譯註：酒），我們的人喝得醉茫茫的，甚至醉到以為看到了『大神』。然後我們的土地就一寸一寸地失掉，我們被趕進樹林裡，離開了湖畔。鷹眼，我連祖墳都沒去拜過。」

「這很悲哀。而我呢，我連個墳墓都不會有，這個臭皮囊就留給野狼吧。你們的族人現在在哪裡？」

「當年夏季裡綻放的那些花去哪裡了？我的族人就像凋謝的花一樣，都去世了。我家族的人都離開了，回到了靈界。眼看就要輪到我了，等到安卡斯也

123

走完我的路時，這個血統也就斷絕了，我的兒子是最後一個摩希根人。

「是誰在講我？」一個聲音說道。

P.21

一個年輕的戰士走過來，跟他們一起坐在溪畔。欽加哥看著兒子，說道：「你在林子裡有發現胡龍人的蹤跡嗎？」

「我發現了十來人左右，都是些膽小鬼，東躲西藏的。」安卡斯說。

「他們想剝頭皮去換錢，他們是孟康的走狗。」鷹眼說。

「我們來把他們趕出樹叢，就像趕鹿一樣。」安卡斯說。

「我有一個更好的想法。我們今晚先好好吃它一頓，明天再去找胡龍人。」鷹眼看看四周，指著遠處的一隻鹿，說道：「我們的晚餐在那裡！」

安卡斯偷偷潛入樹叢，把箭架在弓上，瞄準鹿射過去。

「你們聽，有鹿群走過來。」鷹眼低聲說道。

欽加哥把耳朵貼在地上，說道：「不對，是白人騎著馬往這邊來。」

CHAPTER 3

P.22

何歐看到前方的路上站了個男人，男人的臂上架了一把槍，手指扣住扳機。

「報上名來！」鷹眼問。

「我們是上帝、法律和國王的跟隨者，我們一大早就在樹林裡走，大家都走得很累了，而且我們到現在都還沒吃東西。我們離威廉亨利堡還很遠嗎？」何歐說。

「你們走錯路了，要先沿著河走到愛德華堡才對。」鷹眼說。

「我們今天早上才從愛德華堡出來的。一個印地安人帶我們走到這裡，我們不知道自己現在在哪裡。」何歐說。

「印地安人靠鹿群走的路、天上的星辰和溪流來找路，他們是不可能會迷路的。你們帶路的印地安人是哪個部落的人？」鷹眼說。

「他是胡龍人。」何歐說。

欽加哥和安卡斯跳起身來。

「胡龍人！他們專幹偷雞摸狗的事。你們只帶了一個胡龍人，算你們好運。」鷹眼說。

「帶路的印地安人是由毛火人養大，他叫馬瓜，是我們這邊的人。你還沒回答我們的話，我們離威廉亨利堡還有多遠？」

「我怎麼知道你們不是間諜？」鷹眼問。

P.23

「我是威廉亨利堡的一位軍官，我現在負責護送穆羅上校的女兒——愛麗絲和蔻若——去找上校，我們的印地安嚮導帶我們抄捷徑。」何歐說。

「你們被他唬弄了，他溜走啦。」鷹眼說。

「他沒溜走，他就在我們後面跟著。」何歐說。

「那我倒想見見這個人。」鷹眼說。

鷹眼走進樹叢，他走了沒幾步路，就碰見坐在馬背上焦心等待的兩位女士和

那位傳教士。馬瓜站在後面，身體倚在一棵樹上，鷹眼仔細地打量了他。馬瓜不動聲色，表情冷酷。鷹眼走回何歐旁邊。

「他是胡龍人沒錯，不管是毛火人還是什麼人，都無法改變他。要是我，我一定不會和他一起待在林子裡共度夜晚。我可以親自帶你去愛德華堡，一個小時就可以到，不過你帶了兩位女士，所以也不可能走那麼快。這個林子裡到處都有孟康的戰士，你那個印地安人馬瓜很清楚可以在什麼地方找到他們。馬瓜打算把你們送給法軍，穆羅上校的女兒可是很大的戰利品。」鷹眼回過頭，穿過林樹望向馬瓜站立的地方，接著舉槍瞄準。

P.24

「不要，別射他。」何歐説。

「好吧。」鷹眼説罷，用印地安話和欽加哥、安卡斯低聲商量了一會兒。接著，欽加哥和安卡斯鑽進了樹林裡。

「你走回去和馬瓜説話，讓他分心。」鷹眼對何歐説道。

何歐策馬快步通過樹叢，來到馬瓜休息的地方。

「看來我們離威廉亨利堡還很遠，有一個人可以幫我們帶路。」何歐説。馬瓜睜著眼睛盯著他看。

「那你就不需要我了，我接下來就自己一個人走去威廉亨利堡。」馬瓜説。

「留下來吃點東西，我們明天早上再

動身去堡塞。大家都走得很累了，好好休息一下，明天才有體力上路。」何歐説。

P.25

馬瓜喃喃自語了一下。他從腰間卸下裝肉乾的袋子，開始啃了起來，並且不時地左右張望。

這時，突然傳來一陣窸窣的葉子聲。馬瓜把耳朵轉向聲音傳來的地方。塗上戰紋的安卡斯和父親從樹叢裡走出來，早已準備好開溜的馬瓜，於是一陣風似地跑進林子裡逃走。鷹眼開了一槍，劃出了一道火光。

信任

• 鷹眼和愛麗絲都不信任馬瓜，為什麼？
• 你有過不信任某人的經驗嗎？

CHAPTER 4

P.26

鷹眼、欽加哥和安卡斯從林子裡走出

來，並沒有把馬瓜抓回來。

「他跑得很快，我們沒追上，但我想他吃了我一槍。」鷹眼說。

「他要是中槍了，那就跑不遠。我們去找他，把他逮住。」何歐說。

「朋友，我們要是跟上去，他會把我們引進埋伏裡。你想看到我們的頭皮明天早上掛在孟康的軍帳外面嗎？」鷹眼說。

何歐聽了毛骨悚然，說道：「帶我們走去威廉亨利堡，我會給你酬勞。」

「我們不要酬勞。你們只要一路保持安靜就可以，我們會帶你們到一個隱密的地方，把馬藏起來，這樣馬瓜那邊的人就會找不到我們的足跡。」

他們來到河岸邊，兩個印地安人把藏在樹叢裡的一艘獨木舟搬出來。蔻若、愛麗絲和加慕坐上獨木舟，鷹眼和何歐推著船走進河裡。不久，他們聽到了瀑布的聲音，何歐爬上船的前端，鷹眼則坐在船尾撐篙，避開礁石，讓船順著急流走。

湍急的水流從四面八方沖過來，船上的人嚇得不敢動。突然，獨木舟一個失控被捲入了急流之中，愛麗絲嚇得面如土色，後來船才在一塊岩石邊停了下來。

「你們快爬到岩石上去，在那裡等我。」鷹眼說。

P. 27

他們安全地爬到岩石上，在黑夜裡惶恐地等待著，動也不敢動，生怕摔進了腳下的黑水裡。

沒過多久，鷹眼帶著欽加哥和安卡斯再次出現，還外帶了一隻獵到的小鹿。

「你們有看到那些印地安人嗎？」何歐問。

「我們有看到野狼，這表示那些印地安人在跟蹤我們。這些狼跟在他們後面吃他們吃剩的食物。」鷹眼說。

兩個印地安人跟著鷹眼沿著岩石邊走，三人隨後消失在前方的岩石上。夜裡，何歐和同伴聽到了說話聲，這時亮起一個火光，何歐看到岩壁有一個很深的洞穴，洞口用一塊重重的毯子遮住，鷹眼正拿著一把火炬。

「你們快進來，不要讓胡龍人看到火光了。」鷹眼說。

進了洞穴，鷹眼在火堆上烤著鹿肉，說道：「你們可以放鬆下來。晚餐很簡單，但是很美味喔。」

「這裡安全嗎？」何歐問。

這時欽加哥在洞穴裡掀起另一條毯子，洞穴這一邊也有個洞口，像第一個洞口一樣用毯子蓋住。

「我們像老狐狸一樣，不會待在只有一個洞口的死穴中。這裡很安全，我們的兩邊都是瀑布，我們被河流環繞住。」鷹眼笑道。

P. 28

安卡斯把鹿肉遞給大家。當他要把肉拿給蔻若時，定定地看了她一眼。他有一、兩次溜口說了幾句英語，想引起女士們的注意。鷹眼啖著鹿肉，不時停下來留意遠處是否有可疑的聲音。

「你叫什麼名字？」鷹眼問傳教士。

「加慕，大衛・加慕。」

「好名字。」鷹眼說：「印地安人的名字都很特別，欽加哥的名字是『大蟒蛇』的意思。這不是說他真的像蛇一樣，而是

説他在面對敵人時，會默不作聲、出其不意地進攻。那，加慕先生，你的工作是什麼？」鷹眼問。

名字
- 人們的名字都常具有特別的意思，你叫什麼名字？有什麼特別的意思嗎？
- 你的名字有什麼特別的來源嗎？
- 你的家族裡有人的名字跟你一樣嗎？
- 如果你要取一個印地安名字，你想取什麼樣的名字？

「我是個傳教士。」
「你會用槍嗎？」
「不會。感謝上帝，我不需要用到槍，我只教人唱聖歌。」
「好奇怪的工作。那麼，在我們入睡之前，為我們唱首聖歌如何？」鷹眼問。
「這是我的榮幸。」加慕說。他接著開口唱歌，愛麗絲和蔻若也隨著和聲而唱。唱到一半時，突然傳來一聲駭人的叫聲。
「會不會是那些印地安人看到了我們的火光？」何歐問。

「不可能，這個地方很隱密，他們找不到的。這裡很安全，我們先睡一下吧，明天天亮以前就要出發。」鷹眼說。

CHAPTER 5

P.30

夜裡，他們又聽到叫聲。鷹眼和兩位摩希根人走到洞口外守著，何歐也跟著出去。洞穴外面沁涼如水，聲音是從河流那邊傳來的。
「那是馬的叫聲。附近有狼，馬聞到了狼的氣味。」何歐說。
「我們去對狼群丟個火把，不然早上會沒有馬可以騎。」鷹眼對安卡斯說。在安卡斯還沒動手之前，狼群就發出噪聲，跑進林子裡。
「我們躲起來，靜觀動靜。」鷹眼說
時間慢慢過去，蔻若和愛麗絲互相抱著入睡了，何歐靠在石頭上打盹，加慕躺下去沒多久就呼呼大睡。鷹眼和兩位摩希根人醒著，他們盯著樹林裡和河邊的動靜，留意任何細微的聲響。
天未亮，鷹眼就把何歐叫醒。
「我們該走了。要大家做好準備，等我一把獨木舟拖到岸邊，就下船。」他說。
「抱歉，我睡著了，都沒事吧？」何歐說。
「沒事。」鷹眼說罷，就消失在黑暗中，前去搬獨木舟。
「蔻若！愛麗絲！醒醒！」何歐說。
這時，突然傳來了鬼哭神號的

聲音，兩位女士嚇得驚聲尖叫。加慕站起身來。

「發生什麼事了？」加慕喊道。

P.31

「是印地安人，快趴下！」何歐說。

他們看到河岸邊火光閃閃，砰砰地一陣槍戰。加慕隨即倒在岩石上。看到加慕倒下，岸邊的印地安人發出勝利的叫喊聲。摩希根人向他們開火回去。鷹眼還沒回來，何歐焦急地聽著獨木舟出現的聲響。河流下方傳來了一聲尖叫聲，有一個人被鷹眼的槍射中。印地安人隨之撤退，四周又恢復一片寂靜。

P.33

何歐把加慕移到安全的岩石上。

「他還活著，只有擦到皮肉，他命真大！他下一次就懂得小心啦。」鷹眼說。

「那些印地安人會折返回來嗎？」何歐問。

「會，他們一想好攻擊策略就會回來。」鷹眼問。

他們觀察了一會兒，沒有發現任何動靜。

「我想他們是不會回來

了。」何歐說。

「你不懂胡龍人，他們巴望著我們的頭皮。他們現在掌握了我們的人數和火力，他們會回來的。」鷹眼說。

鷹眼一邊說著，發現了岩石邊躲著幾個印地安人。這時，樹林裡響聲一片喊殺聲。有四個印地安人跑過岩石，又吼又叫。鷹眼和安卡斯拿起槍瞄準，其中兩個人應聲倒下。

鷹眼和何歐一邊衝到岩石下，一邊開著槍。有一個塊頭很大的印地安人持著一把刀朝鷹眼衝過來，兩人搏鬥了起來。鷹眼搶下他的刀子，往他的胸口刺下去。

另一個印地安人向何歐攻過來，兩人在岩石邊打滾。印地安人掐住何歐的脖子，緊緊勒住他的喉嚨，想把他勒死。就在這時，何歐眼前閃過刀片的亮光，接著只見刀子滴下鮮血，那是安卡斯手中的刀。印地安人往後倒在岩石上，手腕上鮮血直冒。

P.34

「在印地安人回來之前，快躲起來！」鷹眼大聲喊道。

鷹眼、何歐和摩希根人鑽進岩石堆裡。那些印地安人氣得又叫又吼，他們開槍，欽加哥也開槍回去，空中一陣颼颼的彈雨。

「讓他們把彈藥用完。安卡斯，小心用，不要浪費子彈。」鷹眼說。

「安卡斯救了我一命！謝謝你，安卡斯，你對我有救命之恩。」何歐握著安卡斯的手說道。

「安卡斯，去獨木舟那裡，把彈藥帶上，會用得到的。」鷹眼説。

然而為時已晚，河裡有一個印地安人正在把船往下流推下去。鷹眼拿起槍瞄準，叩下扳機，槍卻沒有動靜。

「來不及了。我彈藥沒了，船上的彈藥也拿不到了。」鷹眼説。

印地安人發出勝利的叫喊聲。鷹眼一行人聽到林子裡傳來的歡呼聲。

「我們現在怎麼辦？我們會有什麼下場？」何歐問。

鷹眼指著自己的頭說：「我們會失去頭皮。」

「不，你們並不需要犧牲！走吧，你們這些勇敢的人！你們已經做得仁至義盡了，別管我們了，你們快逃命吧！」蔻若説。

「我們順著河水沖下去，也許可以保住小命！」鷹眼説。

「那就試試看吧！」蔻若説。

「穆羅上校要是問起他的女兒，我們要怎麼説？説我們讓印地安人把他們給做了？」鷹眼問。

「你就説，你是為他的女兒們前來求救的，請他盡快趕過來，這樣我們還能得救。」蔻若回答。

P.35

鷹眼和摩希根人用達拉威語商量了一下。欽加哥仔細地聽著，然後把獵刀和戰斧插回腰帶裡，悄悄地走到岩石邊。不一會兒，他跳下水中，消失不見。鷹眼握了一下蔻若的手，接著他把來福槍扔在岩石上，也隨著欽加哥跳進河裡。

蔻若看著安卡斯。

「安卡斯留下來。」這位摩希根人説。

「不，你也要走，你是這樣一個善良大方的人。去找我父親，要他拿錢來贖回他女兒的自由。快走！我要你走！」蔻若説。

安卡斯走過岩石，臨行前又看了蔻若一眼，臉上露出悲傷的神情，然後跟著跳進河裡。

蔻若轉頭看著何歐，跟他説道：「你要跟他們一起走！我們最壞的情況也不過是一死，人早晚都要死的。」

「還有比死更壞的事情，我誓死也不能讓你們受到這種苦。」何歐説。

做出決定
- 為什麼蔻若要鷹眼和兩位摩希根人離開？
- 她做出的決定是正確的嗎？
- 你曾經有過難以做出決定的經驗嗎？那是什麼情況？

印地安人用興奮的語調交談著。

P.36

蔻若沒有和何歐爭論什麼。愛麗絲啜泣了起來，蔻若伸手抱住妹妹，帶她走回洞穴裡。

CHAPTER 6

P.37

印地安人目前還沒有動靜。何歐將加慕扶進洞穴裡。

「我們只能祈禱印地安人找不到我們。」何歐說。

洞裡頭的空氣很清新，加慕的頭還在痛，但是他想開口唱歌。

「印地安人可能會聽到。」蔻若說。

「就讓他唱吧！這裡有瀑布聲，他們聽不到。唱唱歌，會讓我們感覺比較好。」何歐說。

加慕於是放聲高歌，這時洞穴外面傳來了一個叫喊聲。

「他們找到了同伴的屍體，並非是發現我們。」何歐說。

每次只要傳來叫喊聲，何歐都會以為是印地安人發現了他們的藏身之處。何歐聽得到他們的說話聲。

「他們在講什麼？」蔻若小聲問道。

「『La Longue Carabine』，那是法語，指『長來福』，這是他們給鷹眼的外號。他們找到他的槍，以為他死了。」何歐說。

P.38

「他們正在找鷹眼的屍體，這表示鷹眼他們已經逃脫了。等他們找到了魏伯將軍，兩個小時內就會有人來救我們了。」何歐說。

印地安人繼續搜尋，兩位女孩顫抖地緊緊挨坐在一起。沒多久，他們聽到隔壁的洞穴裡清楚地傳來印地安人的聲音。

「別動！」何歐小聲說道。

愛麗絲哭了起來。

「噓！」蔻若說罷，便摟緊妹妹。

洞穴外頭傳來一個叫聲，印地安人隨之跑出洞穴。

「他們找到了另一個屍體。」何歐說。

他們屏息以待，但印地安人沒有再折返回來。

「蔻若，他們走了！愛麗絲，他們回營地了！我們安全了！」何歐說。

愛麗絲鬆了一口氣，臉上恢復了血氣。然而就在她準備開口說話時，突然呆住，臉色剎時又一陣慘白。她盯著洞口，面如死灰。有一個印地安人正往洞裡瞧，他的臉上塗著戰紋。何歐認出了這個人，是馬瓜！

馬瓜沒有立刻看到何歐他們這些人。不一會兒，他的眼睛看到了黑暗的洞穴內部，臉上立刻有了表情——那是勝利的表情。何歐開了一槍，但馬瓜已經消失。

何歐跑到洞口，看到馬瓜沿著一塊狹長的岩石跑去，然後消失不見。在片刻

的寧靜之後，馬瓜發出戰鬥的喊殺聲，其他的印地安人隨即發出駭人的尖叫聲來回應他。

印地安人兵分兩路堵住兩個洞口，何歐他們已經無路可逃。

印地安人把何歐、加慕和兩位女士拖出洞穴，將他們圍住，發出勝利的歡呼聲。

P.39

恐懼

- 你有過害怕的經驗嗎？你害怕什麼？
- 當時是發生了什麼事？
- 你害怕的東西有哪些？把它列出來，和你的夥伴對照一下。

P.40

何歐面對面地和馬瓜對峙著。眼前這個人之前還是他們的嚮導，他們現在卻成了他的階下囚，何歐感到忿忿不平。

「我們族人想要那個獵人——『長來福』鷹眼的命。」馬瓜說。

何歐注意到馬瓜的肩膀上裹著樹葉。

「鷹眼走了！」何歐說。

馬瓜笑笑回答說：「白人以為，死了就可以得到安息，不過我們紅人知道如何折磨敵人的靈魂。鷹眼的屍體在哪裡？我們胡龍人死要見頭皮。」

「鷹眼是逃了，不是死了！」

馬瓜搖搖頭說：「難道他是插翅飛走，或是像魚一樣游走？你少唬弄我們了。」

「他不是魚，但他會游泳。」

「那麼這個白人首領怎麼還留在這裡？你是不想要你的頭皮了嗎？」馬瓜問。

「白人不是膽小鬼，他們不會丟下女人不管。」

馬瓜拉下臉，說道：「難道摩希根人也會游泳？像在灌木叢裡爬行那樣？『大蟒蛇』欽加哥在哪裡？『飛躍的鹿』在那裡？」

「『飛躍的鹿』是誰？」何歐問。

「安卡斯。」馬瓜說。

「這兩個人都沿著河流游走了。」

胡龍人聽不懂何歐在講什麼，他們看著馬瓜，靜待馬瓜為他們解釋。馬瓜指著河流，說了幾句話後，胡龍人失望地叫了一聲。一個胡龍人抓住愛麗絲的頭髮，拿著一把刀子在她的頭旁邊揮來揮去。何歐想出手制止他，但他的雙手被緊縛住。愛麗絲發出驚嚇的尖叫聲。

P.41

「愛麗絲，你冷靜一下，他們只是要嚇嚇你，不會對你怎樣的。」何歐說。

胡龍人指著魏伯軍營的方向大聲叫吼著。他們把這個幾俘虜趕上獨木舟，穿過急流，來到河流的南岸，岸上有其他的胡龍人抓住了馬匹，在那裡等著。大部分的印地安人隨後離開，走進林子裡，留下馬瓜和其他六名胡龍人看管這些俘虜。兩位女士和加慕騎著馬，其他人則是用走的。他們一行人朝著南方出發，這跟前往威廉亨利堡的路是反方向。

蔻若在經過樹木和樹叢時，會隨手抓住樹枝折斷，給鷹眼作暗號。她又趁著沒人看到時，把手套丟在路上，然而這時，一個胡龍人忽然止住她的馬，把掉落的手套撿回來給她，還給她一個凶神惡煞的表情。

CHAPTER 7

P. 42

胡龍人中途停下來歇息時，馬瓜對何歐說：「你去跟穆羅那位黑髮的女兒說，『馬瓜要跟你講話。』」

何歐走到蔻若旁邊。

「他想怎樣？」蔻若問。

「我也不知道，可能想要你父親配合什麼的。」何歐說。

蔻若單獨和馬瓜交談時，一顆心怦怦地跳著，但她仍保持沉著地問道：「馬瓜想要穆羅的女兒怎麼做？你一定要放了我妹妹，我父親要是一次痛失兩個女兒，會活不下去，而且這也不會讓馬瓜因此就感到痛快。」

「只要你答應我一件事，我就放你妹妹走。」馬瓜說。

「你要我答應你什麼事？」蔻若問。

「馬瓜在離開族人時，一個首領霸占了馬瓜的妻子。現在，馬瓜要回到大河邊的祖墳那裡，英國隊長的女兒要跟馬瓜走，一輩子跟著馬瓜住在印地安人的棚子裡。」

P. 43

蔻若一陣哆嗦，這個提議讓她感到噁心。不過她面不改色，不讓馬瓜察覺她的情緒反應。

「難道馬瓜要娶一個和他沒有感情的妻子回家？而且這個妻子的國家和膚色都和他不一樣？你倒不如跟穆羅換黃金，用黃金來擄獲胡龍女人的心還比較實際。」

馬瓜沒有回答，只是直盯著蔻若看。蔻若覺得尷尬，便別過臉去。

馬瓜咬牙切齒地繼續說：「穆羅的女兒要幫馬瓜提水，幫他種田，幫他作飯。馬瓜用這種方式，能讓穆羅心如刀割。」

「你就要讓我父親痛不欲生，只有惡神惡鬼才會想到這種報復的手段。」蔻若大聲喊道。

「走，回去你妹妹那裡。胡龍人有的是方法來折磨你們，你等著瞧！」馬瓜笑道。

蔻若看到胡龍人燒起營火，然後把一根根木樁削尖。他們把兩棵小樹折彎至地面，準備把何歐綁在上頭。蔻若看得膽戰心驚。

P. 44

「穆羅的女兒現在想說什麼嗎？馬瓜的棚子現在還配不上她嗎？她想把自己餵給狼吃嗎？」馬瓜說。

「蔻若，他是什麼意思？」何歐問。

「沒什麼意思。他是野人，不知道自己在做什麼，我們為他禱告，並且寬恕他吧！」蔻若說。

馬瓜指著愛麗絲，說道：「你看！這個小女孩在哭了！她還太小，不能死。

把她送回去給穆羅,她還可以幫穆羅梳梳一頭白髮!」

愛麗絲看著姊姊說:「他這是什麼意思?他要把我放回去給父親?」

「愛麗絲,這個胡龍人不會殺我們的,只要我肯答應他的條件……」蔻若哽住了聲音。

「不要!不要!那我寧願和你同生死!」愛麗絲喊道。

「那你們就送死吧!」馬瓜喊道。他拿起戰斧,朝著愛麗絲猛力擲去,戰斧從何歐的面前呼嘯而過,削掉了愛麗絲的一綹頭髮,斧刀砍進了她頭頂上的樹幹。何歐死命掙斷了綁在手上的枝條。

另一個胡龍人持著戰斧對準愛麗絲,何歐向他撲過去,兩人在地上打成一團。印地安人掙開何歐的手,用膝蓋壓住何歐的胸膛,讓他動彈不得。就在何歐看著印地安人手上的刀子時,忽然傳來一個槍響,印地安人的表情一變,就躺在他身旁斷氣了。

P. 45

胡龍人看到同伴死去,發出一陣怒吼。

「是『長來福』,『長來福』來了!」他們喊道。

這時響起更多的叫囂聲。鷹眼從樹叢中縱身而出,他拾起他的舊來福槍,像執棍棒那樣地在空中揮舞槍支,對著眼前站立的印地安人,朝他們的頭部揮過去。這時有另外一個身影跑過他的身邊,跳進胡龍人裡頭,那是安卡斯,他朝著胡龍人揮動戰斧和獵刀。接著又出現另一個摩希根人,他毫不留情地對胡龍人展開攻擊。

這群受到驚嚇的印地安人高聲喊著「跳躍的鹿」和「大蟒蛇」這兩個名字,然後紛紛躲開這兩個摩希根人。馬瓜掏出獵刀,發出一聲喊殺聲,衝向欽加哥。胡龍人這時和摩希根人及鷹眼展開了白刃戰。安卡斯朝著一個胡龍人跳過去,用戰斧擊向對方的腦門。何歐這時也抓起一把刀子,加入戰局。雙方人馬一番激戰之後,胡龍人非死即傷。

這時,只剩欽加哥和馬瓜還在打鬥,地上揚起陣陣塵煙。他們彼此你來我往,在地上扭做一團,在岩石邊滾來覆去。鷹眼和何歐站在一旁觀戰,一時之間插不上手。鷹眼舉槍瞄向目標,但又作罷。何歐伸手想抓住馬瓜的腳,但沒抓著。安卡斯做好動作準備用獵刀刺馬瓜,但兩人在塵土中翻來滾去,找不到空隙下手。最後,欽加哥終於用刀刺中的馬瓜,馬瓜往後倒在泥土上。欽加哥跳起身來,發出勝利的呼聲。

P. 46

「摩希根人打贏了!」鷹眼叫道。他舉起來福槍,想對著馬瓜的腦門給予最後一擊。然而這時馬瓜翻身滾到岩石邊,鑽進了樹叢裡。摩希根人想乘勝追擊。

「別管他了!」鷹眼叫道。

摩希根人躊躇了一下,沒再追下去。

「別管他了,他現在沒有武器,就像一條沒有牙齒的響尾蛇一樣,傷不了人。我們檢查一下其他人是生是死就好了。」鷹眼說。

愛麗絲在蔻若的懷裡哭喊道:「我們得救了!我們可以回去父親那裡了!謝天謝地!」

「朋友，你們怎麼這麼快就趕過來了？」何歐問鷹眼。

「我們並沒有去堡寨，我們跟蹤你們，伺機而動。」

安卡斯點了營火，張羅著胡龍人留下的食物。

「吃吧，我們還有好長一段路要趕。」鷹眼説。

鷹眼和摩希根人靜靜地把食物吃完，然後到附近的泉水邊喝水。

「我們要出發了。」鷹眼説。

兩位姊妹爬上馬背，何歐和加慕走在後面，鷹眼走在最前面，最後面跟著兩個摩希根人。他們沿著羊腸小徑往北邊走，將胡龍人的屍體留在身後。

CHAPTER 8

P. 48

走了幾個鐘頭後，一群人來到了以前打鬥過的一處地方。

「我和欽加哥曾經在這裡和馬瓜那幫人打過，那是我這輩子第一次出手殺人。我們可以在這裡休息一下。」鷹眼説。

他們擠身穿過叢林，來到一處空地。在空地中央有一個小丘，上面有一個荒廢的房子。愛麗絲和蔻若下了馬，想在沁涼的夜裡好好休息一番。男人們前去檢查了一下房子。

「很少有人知道這個地方。我那時候年紀還很小，但當時殺人流血的畫面，現在還歷歷在目。我們那時候在這裡被困了四十個晝夜，四周都是叫囂的印地安人，等著要我們的命。我後來親手把死者埋起來，就埋在你們現在坐的山丘下。」鷹眼説。

何歐和兩位姊妹一聽，馬上站了起來。

「別怕，他們都死了，不會怎樣的。」鷹眼露出憂傷的神情，對何歐和姊妹們笑了笑。

摩希根人把一座泉水上的樹葉清了清，好讓大家可以飲水。他們又拿了乾樹葉，鋪在廢棄房子的地板上，讓姊妹當床睡。

「欽加哥會幫我們守夜，我們都睡吧。」鷹眼説。

欽加哥在黑夜裡直直坐著不動，不管是姊妹的呼吸聲，還是夜風吹動樹葉的窸窣聲，再微小的聲音都逃不過他的耳朵。

何歐沉睡之後，有一個人輕拍了他的肩膀，把他喚醒。他立刻跳了起來。

P. 49

「你是誰？是敵還是友？」何歐説。

「我是朋友。」那是欽加哥的聲音。欽

加哥指著月亮說：「月亮出來了，白人的堡寨還很遠，我們該走了。」

鷹眼帶著眾人安全通過樹林，他對這一帶看起來瞭若指掌。他們朝著山區走去，路面變得愈來愈崎嶇。

這時，鷹眼忽然停住腳步。

「小心，這附近有軍隊駐紮。」鷹眼小聲說道。

「我們一定是快到威廉亨利堡了。」何歐說。

「不要出聲，緊緊跟著我。」鷹眼說。

他們走沒多久，就看到有一個人朝著他們走過來。

「大家把武器準備好。」鷹眼說。

「是誰？」一個說法語的聲音說。

危險

• 你想，朝他們走過來的人是誰？
• 為什麼鷹眼要大家把武器準備好？
• 你有遇到過什麼驚險的情況嗎？
• 你當時的感覺是什麼？想像一種危險的情況，跟夥伴分享彼此的想法。

P.50

鷹眼沒有作聲。

「是誰？」那個聲音又問了一次。

這時何歐用法語回應，說出了通關密碼「France」（法蘭西）。

「你是國王手下的軍官？」哨兵又問。

「是，我是。我帶來了穆羅上校的女兒，他們被我綁來了，我準備把他們交給將軍。」何歐用道地的法語說。

哨兵向何歐和女士們指

出到軍營的路。沒多久，他們聽到身後傳來一聲長長的呻吟聲。

「那是什麼聲音？」愛麗絲問。

「你應該問『那是誰的聲音？』」鷹眼說。

何歐環顧四周，發現欽加哥不見了。他們這時又聽到另一聲呻吟聲，接著是有東西重重落入水裡的聲音。

P.51

一會兒後，欽加哥才從樹叢裡走出來。

鷹眼很快帶著一行人來到了一處高地，在岩崖邊可以看到湖岸和威廉亨利堡的建築物，在堡寨的附近，還可以看到一個軍營。

「你們看一下南邊，有看到從樹林裡竄起的煙火嗎？那就是敵人所在的方位。」鷹眼說。

在湖的南岸，可以看到一些白色的帳篷，和一個很大的兵備營帳。

「你想他們有多少兵力？」何歐問。

「有一萬名兵力左右。」鷹眼問。

就在他們觀察之際，山谷裡傳來了轟轟的砲火聲，東邊的山丘隨即響起一陣回音。一行人繼續朝著堡寨對面的平野前進。湖面上籠罩著濃霧。這時他們又聽到一個法軍哨兵說：「是誰在那裡？」

「繼續走！」鷹眼小聲說。

這時傳來了更多聲音，用法語說道：「是誰在那裡？」

「繼續走！」何歐重複道。

接著他叫了一聲：「是我！」

「你是誰？」對方問。

「我是法軍這邊的人。」何歐説。

「你是法軍的敵人！」一個法國士兵喊道。

接著傳來更多士兵的聲音，還有一聲「開火！」的軍令。

頓時，五十把槍朝著濃霧齊射，子彈呼嘯而落，但鷹眼一行人走的是另一個方向。

P.52

「我們反擊回去，這樣他們會以為遭受攻擊，就會撤退等待支援。」鷹眼説。

這個盤算很如意，只可惜並未奏效。法軍一聽到槍擊聲，立即派了更多的士兵前來。

「我們快逃，等一下整支軍隊就會圍過來了。」何歐説。

這時閃起一道光芒，砲火轟轟地朝平野這邊投射過來。

「我們往堡寨跑！」鷹眼説。

他們一行人往堡寨的方向跑去，安卡斯牽著蔻若的手跑，後面傳來士兵尾隨的聲音。這時，他們聽到堡寨內傳出一個講話的聲音。

「預備！看到敵人，就發射！」

愛麗絲一聽，立刻認出了這個聲音。

「爸爸！爸爸！我是愛麗絲，快救我們啊！快救救你的女兒！」愛麗絲喊道。

「別開火！是我女兒！快，打開寨門！別開火！用刀劍備戰！」穆羅説。

堡寨內隨即衝出一群士兵，何歐也加入他們，和他們一起對抗法軍。蔻若和愛麗絲被單獨留在那裡，嚇得渾身顫抖。不一會兒，一名年長的軍官跑向她們，張開雙臂緊緊抱住她們。軍官的眼淚撲漱漱地掉下來，用著蘇格蘭腔調喊道：「感謝上帝！讓我的女兒平安無事！」

CHAPTER 9

P.53

圍城之戰持續了幾天，穆羅上校盡一切力量抵擋法軍的攻擊。堡寨四周的林子裡都是孟康手下的印地安戰士，他們無法突破重圍。魏伯將軍也沒有加派兵力過來，彷彿這個堡寨已經被遺忘。

在那段驚險萬分的護送旅程結束之後，何歐就沒有再見過蔻若和愛麗絲。到了第五天，他才看到她們正和父親沿著堡寨的城牆邊走過。她們的人看起來精神煥發。

「何歐少校，我們都還沒有機會跟你道謝，你救了我們的命！」蔻若説。

「何歐少校，我需要你另外幫我一件事。」穆羅上校説。

「是什麼事？」何歐説。

幫忙

- 你遇到困難時，會找人幫忙嗎？
- 你會找誰幫忙？
- 你自己會幫忙別人嗎？
- 常常有別人找你幫忙嗎？
- 設想一些你求助於別人，以及你對別人伸出援手的情況，描繪一下狀況。

P.55

穆羅對何歐講了一些話，片刻之後，何歐便走在前往孟康軍營的路上。一位法國軍官帶他來到指揮官的營帳。這位法國指揮官的身邊圍繞著法國軍官、不同部落的印地安酋長和戰士，這時何歐也看到了馬瓜那張邪門的臉正盯著他看。他停下腳步，孟康跟他打了招呼。

「您代表穆羅上校長官前來，我深表歡迎！」孟康説。

何歐向孟康深深一鞠躬。孟康沉默了一會，説道：「何歐少校，你知道我方的兵力嗎？」

「確切的數字我們並不清楚，我們估計最多不會超過兩萬人。」何歐答道。

這個法國指揮官細細地打量了何歐的表情。何歐給的數字，比實際的人數多了兩倍。孟康繼續説：「那麼，您是來跟我談投降的條件的嗎？」

「我想，威廉亨利堡的軍力，閣下並不知情。」何歐説。

「我看威廉亨利堡只有兩千三百名士兵。」孟康説。

「威廉亨利堡蓋在河邊，蓋得很牢固，而且在離我們幾小時路程的地方，還有一支強大的軍隊。」何歐説。

P.56

「那也不過只有六千到八千名的士兵，而且魏伯將軍認為，要把他們派來這裡，不如讓他們駐守愛德華堡。」孟康説。

他們談判結束後，何歐起身告辭。孟康彬彬有禮的態度，讓他印象深刻。然而他對於敵方軍力的情況，一無所獲。

禮貌

- 在我們今天這個社會裡，「禮貌」很重要嗎？舉一些例子來說明「禮貌」與「不禮貌」的行為。和夥伴討論一下，你在面對以下的情況時，通常會做何反應？
  a. 你在一家商店前面等著買東西，但你的前面正大排長龍。
  b. 你在公車上正坐得舒服，這時有一個老者上了車。
  c. 你想找某人，而對方房間的門是關閉著的。

回到堡寨後，何歐向穆羅報告了談判的結果。

「魏伯將軍正派軍隊過來支援我們，我說什麼都不會把堡寨交出去。」穆羅上校説。

投降與否的討論定案之後，何歐趁這個機會提了另一件事情。

「我有個不情之請。」何歐説。

「我大概知道你要說什麼。」穆羅説。

「不知我是否有這個榮幸，能做您的半子？」何歐説。

「何歐，你這個話講得很明白，那你是否也對我的女兒這樣明白地吐露過？」穆羅説。

P.57

「還沒有。您這麼信任我，我不能濫用您的信任。」何歐説。

「何歐少校，你算是個君子。但是蔻若很聰明，不用我這個做父親的來保護她。」

「蔻若？」何歐説。

「是呀，是蔻若！我們在談你對穆羅小姐的情意，不是嗎？」

「我……想我並沒有提到她的名字。」何歐説。

「那你想娶的是哪一位？」穆羅説。

「您的另一個女兒，她長得也是一樣漂亮。」

「你是説愛麗絲？」穆羅説。

穆羅説：「我應該讓你了解一下我的過去。我出身一個蘇格蘭的貴族家庭，但這個家庭並不富裕。我在你這個年紀的時候，遇到了一位叫做愛麗絲・葛漢的女子，她是一個土財主的女兒。我向她求婚，但他父親反對。後來，我投身軍旅，離開英國，去海外為國王服役。我到過很多地方，打過很多戰爭，後來被派到西印度群島。我在那裡遇到了我的妻子，也就是蔻若的母親。我的妻子是一位紳士的女兒，但她的祖先曾經當過奴隸。在很多地方，奴隸所生的孩子都會被瞧不起。」

P.58

「這種事非常不幸。」何歐説。

「你大概以為我的女兒蔻若配不上你。」穆羅説。

「我想我永遠也不會有這種可恥的偏見！但我愛上的是您小女兒愛麗絲的甜美可愛。」何歐説。

「愛麗絲和她媽媽可以説是同一個模子印出來的。在蔻若的母親過世之後，我回到蘇格蘭，我沒想到的是，我心愛的人竟然沒有結婚！她痴心守了我二十年，而我卻娶了別人，把她給忘了。我回來之後，她原諒了我，而且嫁給了我。」穆羅説。

「她就是愛麗絲的母親？」何歐問。

「是的，正是！只是，我和她只有一年的夫妻緣份，她就過世了。」穆羅説著，不禁泣數行下。「我們別説這個了，我們要討論孟康的事。」

穆羅同意由何歐陪同去會晤法軍指揮官。孟康和上次一樣，表現得溫文有禮，親切地歡迎他們。孟康説法文，由何歐翻譯。

「請轉述給穆羅上校知道，他和他的士兵英勇奮戰，然而到了這種時刻，應該棄械投降。我方兵力強大，要擊敗我們是不可能的。」

「我知道法軍很強大，但我們的國家也擁有很多忠心耿耿的士兵。」穆羅説。

P.59

「可惜遠水救不了近火。」孟康用英語説。

「原來閣下也諳通英語。」何歐説。

「閣下，請原諒。對於外國語言，能説和能聽，差別很大。請繼續翻譯。」孟康説。

138

外國語言

- 你會說幾種不同的語言？
- 你覺得學習外國語言很困難嗎？
- 孟康說：「對於外國語言，能說和能聽，差別很大。」你想他是指什麼？

孟康又說：「我們從這些山丘上可以清楚地偵察到你們動靜，所以我們確切掌握了你們的軍力。」

「您的望遠鏡能看到哈德遜河嗎？您難道沒看到魏伯將軍正派軍隊過來嗎？」穆羅說。

P.61

「我看未必盡然。」孟康說道，一邊遞了一封信給穆羅。

穆羅沒等何歐翻譯孟康的話，逕自接過信來看。之後，只見他淚裡噙著淚水，信紙從他手中滑落，彷彿一切希望都破滅了的樣子。何歐隨即撿起信紙起來讀。

信中，魏伯將軍勸穆羅投降，並且說他不會派一兵一卒去支援他。

「這封信是真的，這是魏伯的親筆簽名沒錯。」何歐說。

「他出賣了我。」穆羅說。

「我們現在還擁有堡寨，我們還擁有我們的榮譽！」何歐說。

「謝謝你，你提醒了我應盡的職責。我們回去堡寨，掘好我們的墳墓，和堡寨共存亡。」穆羅說。

「先生們，在你們離開之前，請聽聽我的條件。我保證，你們的投降將保有尊嚴。」孟康說。

穆羅思索了半晌，說道：「何歐，你就和孟康將軍談判投降的事吧。我活了這麼大一把歲數，我見識到了兩件事：一個英國人竟會嚇得不敢出兵救援自己的戰友，而一個法國人卻這樣正直，不利用自己的有利地位來迫害他人。」

穆羅回到堡寨，大家都看得出來他帶回來的是壞消息。經過這次的挫敗，穆羅一蹶不振。何歐談妥投降條件，穆羅簽署了投降書，同意於次日早午交出堡寨。英軍可以保有自己的武器、軍旗等一切輜重，也因而保住了榮譽。

CHAPTER 10

P.62

清晨之際，孟康走出軍帳，空氣峭寒。

「是誰在那裡？」一個哨兵問。

「我是孟康將軍。」

「大人，您早！請好走。」哨兵說。

孟康朝著威廉亨利堡的西面走去，這時傳來一個聲響，馬瓜持著一把來福槍，瞄準孟康的頭部。

「你這是在做什麼？戰事結束了。」孟康說。

印地安人用法語回答他說：「沒有一個戰士獵到頭皮，而白人卻成了朋友！」

馬瓜說罷，轉頭走掉，孟康則走回軍營。

在法軍的軍營裡，一片號角聲響起。今天是投降日，堡寨外，陽光燦爛，法軍整好隊伍，聽取命令。在堡寨內，則是另一番情景。婦女小孩準備離開，士兵默不作聲地排成縱隊，穆羅神情憂悒地站在眾人面前。

蔻若和愛麗絲望著士兵步行走出堡寨，法軍此時接管了堡寨的大門。何歐走在最前面，領著部隊離開，這時，蔻若聽到了一個熟悉的叫喊聲。一時之間，不知從哪裡冒出了近百名的印地安人，蔻若在當中瞧見了馬瓜的身影。馬瓜對著胡龍人大喊，發號施令。

P.63

一群婦女走出堡寨。其中有一個母親，她披著一條色彩鮮艷的圍巾，手裡抱著一個小孩。一個胡龍人走過去，想搶下她的圍巾，她連忙拿圍巾裹住小孩。胡龍人把孩子搶過來，圍巾掉落地上，另一個胡龍人隨手把圍巾撿起來。這位母親嚇得驚聲尖叫。

這時，馬瓜用手拍著嘴部，發出胡龍人的喊殺聲。一聽到這個信號，樹林裡衝出了兩千多名印地安人。他們瘋狂地屠殺，獵取敵人的頭皮。他們殺得血流成河，士兵想反擊，槍匣裡卻沒有子彈。

愛麗絲和蔻若手足無措地看著眼前的場面，加慕守在她們身邊。周圍是一片死傷的慘叫聲。愛麗絲看到父親穿過印地安人，朝著法國軍營走去。胡龍人對著穆羅揮舞長矛，穆羅將矛撥開。胡龍人不敢動這種重要的角色人物。

P.64

「爸爸！爸爸！我們在這裡！」愛麗絲尖叫著，但穆羅沒有注意到她們。愛麗絲昏厥倒地，蔻若想把她搖醒。

「我們找機會逃出去！」加慕說。

「不！你先走！你自己先逃命要緊！」蔻若看著妹妹說。

加慕站起身子，開始放開嗓子唱歌。他歌聲嘹亮，在一片喧囂聲中，印地安人還能聽到他的歌聲。有幾個胡龍人衝到他們的前面，想取他們的頭皮，然而當他們看到加慕在唱歌時，就改變了想法，轉而離開，兩位姊妹也因此保住了性命。

馬瓜聽到加慕的歌聲，便跑來他們的面前。

「來！」他對蔻若說。

「不要碰我！」蔻若喊道。

馬瓜聽了哈哈大笑，他舉起沾滿鮮血的手，說道：「這個血是紅色的，但這是從白人身上流出來的。」

「你是個妖魔鬼怪！這都是你一手造成的。」蔻若喊道。

「馬瓜是一個偉大的酋長！黑髮女士要跟他回部落嗎？」馬瓜說。

「你休想！你不是要報仇嗎？你現在就殺了我！」蔻若說。

馬瓜躊躇了一下。接著他抱起愛麗絲，朝林子裡跑去。

「你別跑！放開她！」蔻若跟在後面，大聲喊道。

馬瓜沒有理會她。加慕跟在蔻若後面，拉高嗓門唱歌。他們兩人就這樣一

路穿越過平野，四周都是傷者、死者，和拚死逃命的人。

P. 66

馬瓜一路來到馬匹的旁邊。她示意蔻若坐上馬背，然後把愛麗絲放到蔻若的馬上，自己牽著馬走向樹林。加慕坐上另一匹馬，尾隨在後。

他們行走了一段時間，來到山頂上的一塊平地。在這裡，他們看到堡寨外的那片平野到處都是屍體。遠方的屠殺持續進行，愛麗絲和蔻若可以聽到傷者的叫喊聲。過了不久，就只剩下印地安人的歡呼聲。

在大屠殺後的第三天，堡寨四周一片死寂。印地安人已經撤走了，堡寨內空無一人，堡寨被燒成焦土。

向晚時分，只見一行五個人——鷹眼、兩位摩希根人、穆羅和何歐——他們從林子裡出來，朝著堡寨走去。他們檢查屍體，只希望不會在屍堆裡找到愛麗絲和蔻若。安卡斯從樹叢上拉下一個東西，拿著它對同伴揮舞著，那是蔻若綠色面紗的一角。這個小小的線索顯示兩位姊妹可能還活著。

P. 67

「我的孩子啊！把我的孩子還給我！」穆羅喊道。

「安卡斯會盡力而為。」安卡斯說。

欽加哥指著一個腳印。

「這是他們的足跡，他們被印地安人擄走了！」何歐說。

「我保證，我們一定找得到他們。這是鹿皮鞋的腳印，安卡斯，你說是不是？」鷹眼說。

這個年輕的摩希根人察看了一下足跡。

「是馬瓜的腳印。」安卡斯說。

「沒錯，馬瓜和黑髮女士曾經走過這裡。」鷹眼表示同意地說。

「那愛麗絲呢？」何歐問。

「這裡沒有她的線索。」鷹眼說。他觀察周圍的樹木和樹叢，又說：「那邊刺叢上有個東西。」

安卡斯走過去細瞧之後，帶著加慕的校音笛走回來。

「他故意留下這個線索給我們，他比我想還要聰明。安卡斯，找找這位傳教士的腳印吧。」鷹眼說。

天色漸自暗了，他們一行人走回堡寨的廢墟。

「我們先休息，等明天早上有精神了再繼續搜尋。」鷹眼說。

線索
- 他們如何判斷蔻若還活著？請找出三條線索。
- 和夥伴設計一個短程的尋寶活動，寫下線索，考考另一組夥伴。

CHAPTER 11

P. 68

「跟著我走，小心腳要踩在石頭或碎木

頭上。」鷹眼說。

其他人聽了照辦。

「這樣我們就不會留下足跡。草地上會留下腳印，在石頭或木頭上就不會。最好不要穿軍靴，鹿皮鞋才不會留下腳印，而且比較好走。」鷹眼說。

到了湖邊，安卡斯小心翼翼地把獨木舟推進河裡，不讓沙灘上留有腳印。他們一行人坐上船，由摩希根人駕槳離開堡寨。

破曉時分，他們穿越湖泊，來到小島群一帶。印地安人有可能埋伏在這裡，所以他們一路上靜悄悄地通過。欽加哥指著天邊從一座島上升起的雲霧。

「那是炊煙。」鷹眼說。

他們在那座島的北岸發現了兩艘獨木舟。

「他們還沒有發現我們，我們快走。」鷹眼說。

然而就在鷹眼說完話的當下，就傳來了一聲槍聲。胡龍人發現了他們。胡龍人跑向他們自己的獨木舟，將船推進湖裡。鷹眼和摩希根人繼續划槳，迅速地往前移動。

「我們的船就跟他們保持這樣一定的距離，他們的子彈打不到我們。」鷹眼說罷，便把槳放下，然後舉起長來福槍瞄準敵方。

鷹眼等著對方的獨木舟進入他的射程範圍，然而就在他開火之前，又來了另一艘獨木舟。他們接著競逐起來，胡龍人拚命划近鷹眼的船，但離他們還是在射程之外。

P.69

「我們進入了他們的射線。」何歐說。

欽加哥發出一聲摩希根人的喊殺聲。胡龍人大喊著鷹眼和兩位摩希根人的綽號：「長來福！大蟒蛇！跳躍的鹿！」

鷹眼對著胡龍人揮舞著長來福槍，胡龍人反擊，但子彈只能落在湖面上。接著輪到鷹眼瞄準放槍，只見獨木舟最前端的印地安人應聲往後倒下，手上的槍支落進了水裡。鷹眼和摩希根人趁著一陣混亂，加緊划船把距離拉開。

他們駛進寬闊的湖面，兩邊是挾湖的高山。他們整齊劃一的划著槳，在何歐看來，鷹眼和兩位摩希根人好像把這種競速當成比賽似的。欽加哥將獨木舟對著山丘那邊的提空卓堡駛進，胡龍人遠遠被他們拋在後面，看來已經放棄追擊。接下來的幾個鐘頭，鷹眼留意他們可能的動靜，最後他們來到了湖的北岸。

湖岸的水面上有濃密的樹叢，他們在樹叢的掩護下前進，直到鷹眼認為可以安全登陸。他們在船上待到天色轉暗，然後才再度啟程，朝著西岸悄聲前進。掌舵的安卡斯讓船安全登上了岸。

P. 70

實用的技能

• 你知道什麼實用的技能，能夠幫助你在野外求生，就像鷹眼和摩希根人那樣？從下列清單中勾選你會的技能。

☐ 划獨木舟　☐ 游泳　☐ 騎馬
☐ 升火　☐ 捕魚　☐ 煮飯
☐ 使用指南針　☐ 長途步行
☐ 攀登岩石
☐ 由星斗的方位來判斷方向

　他們把船扛進林子，藏在樹枝下。不一會兒，他們拾起槍支和緇重，開始了下一段的行程。

CHAPTER 12

P. 71

　鷹眼領著大家來到一塊荒蠻之地。安卡斯觀察地上的足跡，然後指著地上，上面有被新翻起不久的泥土，看來像是有大型的動物最近剛走過這裡。

　「找到足跡了！什麼蹤跡都逃不過安卡斯的眼睛。」鷹眼說。

　到了下午，他們來到了馬瓜一行人歇過腳的地方。胡龍人在這裡升了火烤肉，吃剩的骨頭散了四處。馬匹也在這裡吃了樹葉，還有人在樹叢下鋪了

個睡覺的地方，何歐認為蔻若和愛麗絲就在那裡睡過。他們繼續悄然前進，最後來到了山丘旁。

　「我聞到胡龍人的味道了，他們的營地就在附近。欽加哥，你抄右邊。安卡斯，你抄左邊，沿著溪走。我跟著足跡前進，誰要是遇到狀況，就叫三聲烏鴉的聲音。」鷹眼說。

　摩希根人各自分頭離開，鷹眼和何歐、穆羅繼續往前走。

　「你們先去樹林邊待著，等我的消息。」鷹眼對何歐說。

P. 72

　何歐藏身在樹叢裡，眼前的景象讓他大開眼界。在湖岸邊和湖水中，佇立了一百多個印地安棚子。這時傳來了一陣樹葉的沙沙聲，在他前面不遠的地方，出現了一個印地安人，何歐按住不敢動。這個印地安人臉上雖然塗著彩紋，但他的樣子看起來不但不凶狠，而且還一副很憂愁的樣子。他正觀察著這位印地安人時，鷹眼溜到了身旁。

　「你看，我們發現了他們的營地，這裡有一個印地安人！」何歐說。

　「他不是胡龍人，他穿著白人的衣服。」鷹眼看著那個人說。

　鷹眼潛到那個人的後面，何歐在一旁看著。鷹眼沒有抓住他，而是伸手拍拍他的肩膀，低聲說：「朋友，你在這

143

裡做什麼？你現在是在教水獺唱歌嗎？」

「沒錯，難道牠們就不能學唱歌嗎？」

「是加慕！」何歐說。

P.73

「女士們在哪裡？」鷹眼問。

男士們圍著加慕，迫不及待想聽他說。

「他們被胡龍人關起來了，不過人都很安全，毫髮未傷。」加慕說。

「兩個人都沒事？」何歐問。

「是的，兩個人都沒事。他們走了很辛苦的一段路，吃的也很少，但除此之外，一切安好。」

「謝天謝地！我要趕快去把我的孩子找回來！」穆羅說。

「這不行！那個胡龍人頭子像惡神惡鬼一樣可怕。他今天帶手下去打獵，把愛麗絲交給附近不遠地方的胡龍族婦女看管，蔻若則被帶到山頭那一邊的一個村落裡。那邊的印地安人也是往孟康那邊靠的。」

P.74

「那你為什麼可以自由行動？」何歐問。

「他們好像很喜歡我的歌聲，所以准許我自由出入。」加慕說。

「好，那你回去跟愛麗絲說我們人已經來了。」鷹眼說。

「我跟他一起去。我就裝得瘋瘋癲癲的，你們幫我喬裝一下，看是要塗彩紋還是什麼的，都行。」何歐說。

欽加哥負責幫忙偽裝，他在何歐的臉上塗上印地安人正統的彩紋，給他畫了一個開心果的滑稽表情。

「畫得太妙了！」欽加哥畫完之後，鷹眼說道。

「我現在看起來怎樣？」何歐問。

「你現在要是用法語和他們講話，他們會以為你是提空卓堡來的雜耍藝人，是結盟部落的人。現在，就開始進行我們的計畫。」鷹眼說。

CHAPTER 13

P.75

在村落的中央有一個樹枝蓋成的棚屋，這是部落召開會議的地方。加慕和何歐朝著棚屋走去，棚屋四周有一群印地安小孩。兩名站在兩旁的戰士放他們進入。敵人就近在眼前，何歐不禁打了個哆嗦。他跟隨加慕進入棚屋，力作鎮定。他們不發一語，在棚屋裡坐下來。他們身邊就坐著一些戰士，在等著他們開口說話。在他們對面，則坐了三、四個德高望重的酋長。

這時，一個酋長打破沉默，說：「我們聽說，加拿大人對自己的白臉感到很驕傲，難道他們現在也開始塗起彩紋了？」

「印地安酋長去找白人弟兄時，會換下皮衣，換上送來的襯衫。我的弟兄現在

為我塗上彩紋，所以我就這麼來了。」何歐說。

穿著

• 遇到下列情況，你會如何穿著打扮？
　□找朋友　　□家庭聚會
　□去上學　　□打工面試

P.76

一個上了年紀的酋長做了個讚許的手勢，其他的同伴也都發出了一聲歡呼。何歐鬆了一口氣，正當他要開口講話時，外面傳來了尖叫聲。

戰士立即起身走出棚屋，何歐和加慕尾隨在後。外面有一些印地安人在大聲吶喊呼叫，從樹林那邊走出來了一排戰士，正往棚屋走過來。

戰士們拔出獵刀在空中揮舞，他們排成兩行，中間留出一個走道。男孩們從父親的腰帶上抽出戰斧，鑽進走道裡，擺出和父親一樣的姿勢。在行伍的最後面有一個俘虜，他站得直挺挺的，準備英勇地面對自己的命運。這時，一個吶喊聲令下，印地安人開始大聲地叫囂吶喊。

俘虜在印地安行列中像鹿一樣迅速地跑走，印地安人還來不及對他下手，他便從一排孩子的頭頂跳過，往林子的方向跑去。印地安人追過去，差點抓到他。他掉頭往另一個方向跑，想再逃進樹林裡。這是他最後的掙扎。

有一個身材高大、孔武有力的胡龍人追過去，一邊揮舞著手中的戰斧，就在這時，何歐把腳伸出去，將他絆倒，那位俘虜趁機逃走。何歐抬眼一看，只見俘虜站在屋前一根繪有彩紋的小柱子旁，不發一語。那裡是聖壇，人們不能靠近，俘虜的命運現在要等胡龍人開會來做決定。一直到了這時候，何歐才看清楚俘虜的臉。那是安卡斯。

P.77

一個戰士抓住安卡斯的手臂，把他押進棚屋裡。酋長和重要的戰士跟在後面，何歐也跟著混進去。安卡斯沉著地站在棚屋的中間。

酋長對安卡斯說：「摩希根人，你已經證明了自己是個男子漢，我現在邀請你跟我們一起吃飯，做我們胡龍人的朋友。你可以休息到明天早上，到時候我們會再對你做出最後的決定。」

這時，來了一個老婦人，她走向俘虜，繞著安卡斯緩緩舞動，在安卡斯的臉旁揮動火把，口中唸著咒語。安卡斯不屈不卑地站著，他凝視著前方，不理會婦人。

勇敢

• 有什麼歷史人物是你覺得很勇敢的？
• 他們做了哪些事？
• 你自己曾經做過什麼勇敢的事嗎？是什麼事？
• 你曾經像故事中的安卡斯那樣地勇敢嗎？

P.78

這時，門口出現了一個黑色的身影。他走進棚屋，靜靜地在印地安人之間走動，然後在何歐的旁邊坐下。何歐瞥了他一眼，不禁嚇得毛骨悚然。坐在他旁邊的人，正是馬瓜。

馬瓜沒有注意到何歐。他盯著安卡

一條羊腸小徑。就在他們開始準備穿越一片草地時，前方突然出現了一個巨大的黑色身影，擋住了他們的路。那是一隻大熊。何歐記得，印地安人有時會馴養熊當寵物，但即使如此，要保持鎮定也是很困難的。這隻大熊就跟在他們的後面。

P. 80

寵物
- 有些人就像印地安人那樣，會養奇奇怪怪的動物來當寵物。問問你的夥伴，會不會想要養下面這些動物？請他們說明理由。
  □鱷魚　□蛇　□蜘蛛
  □熊　　□老鼠
- 你能想出還有哪些奇怪的寵物嗎？
- 你覺得哪些動物是最佳的寵物？

他們來到一個洞穴口，酋長推開木門，走進狹長的甬道裡。那隻大熊還繼續跟著他們，牠對何歐咆哮了一、兩次，想用大熊掌碰他。

洞穴裡有好幾個房間，當中一個房間裡躺著一個臥病的婦女。

「待在這個地方，邪靈就比較找不到她。」酋長說。

生病婦女的床邊圍著一群印地安婦人，而加慕就站在她們的中間。何歐看了一下婦女，發現自己愛莫能助，因為婦女看起來全身癱瘓。

加慕開始唱起聖歌，旁邊卻傳來一種人不像人、鬼不像鬼的聲音。加慕警覺地環顧四周，看到洞穴的一個黑暗角落裡坐著那隻大熊。大熊的身體左右搖晃

斯，對空揮拳，手鐲上的銀環發出咯咯聲響。他憤怒地吼道：「摩希根人，你死定了！」

馬瓜站起身來，舉著戰斧在頭頂揮舞，然後將戰斧擲出。戰斧在空中飛過，被火把照得閃閃發光，滑過安卡斯頭頂上的髮絲。

安卡斯紋風不動地站著，目光直視著敵人的眼睛。

「把他帶下去！明天一早他就死定了！」馬瓜說。

年輕的戰士隨即把安卡斯押出屋外，馬瓜跟著走出去。

酋長這時抽完菸，他示意何歐跟他出去。

「陌生人，來吧！我手下有人的妻子中邪了，你是巫醫，就由你來驅鬼吧！」酋長說。

他們朝著附近的山腳走去，接著步入

著，並且發出低吼聲，像是在模仿加慕的歌聲一樣。加慕嚇得不敢再唱下去，他轉向何歐，很快地小聲說道：「愛麗絲就在附近，她正在等你。」說罷，他就跑出房間。

P. 81

胡龍人酋長要婦女們離開。

「現在，就看看我的弟兄怎麼驅魔吧！」他一邊說著，一邊指著生病的婦女。

何歐口中唸唸有詞，佯裝在為婦女持咒。這時大熊發出一個凶猛的叫聲，打斷了他。

「是鬼魂在嫉妒。」酋長說。

酋長轉向大熊，對牠說：「靜下來！」然後又轉向何歐說：「我出去。」

現在洞穴裡只剩下何歐和生病的婦女，還有一隻猛獸。大熊走向何歐，在他前面坐下。何歐眼睜睜看著大熊，心想自己隨時會被攻擊。大熊的身體這時搖晃起來，用大熊掌搓著自己的臉，突然，熊的頭部倒向一旁，在原來的頭部部位出現了鷹眼的臉。

CHAPTER 14

P. 82

「我們分開之後，我和安卡斯去了另一個營地。你有看到他嗎？」鷹眼說。

「他被胡龍人給抓了，他們準備明天天一亮，就將他處死。」何歐說。

「我不會讓胡龍人得逞！」鷹眼繼續說出他們遇到的事，「我們撞見了一幫胡龍人，其中有一個膽小鬼，拔腿就逃。安卡斯追著他到了營地，結果被印地安人抓住了。我射了兩個胡龍人，來到村落附近。後來我碰見一個從村落走出來的巫醫，他當時披著這件熊皮，我就把它奪過來。現在，我們有活要幹了。你知道愛麗絲在哪裡嗎？」

「我在村落裡四處都找過，就是沒有看到她的蹤跡。」何歐說。

「你聽到加慕講了，他說愛麗絲就在這附近等著你。」鷹眼說。

他們兩個人在洞穴裡找尋愛麗絲的身影。何歐看到遠處有燈光在閃爍，便驅前探個究竟。他看到一個房間裡塞滿了從威廉亨利堡劫來的物品，在房間的中央，就坐著愛麗絲。愛麗絲看起來很蒼白，受到了驚恐，但美麗如昔。

「我就知道你不會拋下我不管！」愛麗絲喊道。

何歐跪在她身邊，說道：「多虧有鷹眼這個朋友的幫忙，我們可以從這些野蠻人的手中逃出去。你一定要勇敢一點！」這時，有一個人輕拍他的肩膀，打斷他的話。他跳起身來轉過頭去，眼前站著的這個人，是馬瓜。

P. 83

這個胡龍人用嘲諷的態度，對著他們這兩個年輕人哈哈大笑。

「馬瓜是一個偉大的酋長！」

147

現在我們就來看看，白人能如何勇敢地對嚴刑拷打一笑置之。」馬瓜説。

就在馬瓜準備離開之際，傳來了一聲吼叫。門口出現了一隻大熊的身影。大熊左右搖晃，然後突然向馬瓜伸出兩隻胳臂，緊緊抱住他的肩膀。

馬瓜死命掙扎，但他的手臂被鷹眼緊緊地挾住。何歐從成捆的木柴堆上扯下一些皮繩，把馬瓜的手臂、大腿和腳綑住，再用一塊布綁住他的嘴巴，讓他無法出聲。他們讓馬瓜躺在地上，留在洞穴裡動彈不得。

「我們現在快走吧！」鷹眼説。

「愛麗絲昏過去了！」何歐説。

「別擔心，用印地安毯子把她裹住，你只要抱她跟著我走就行，接下來的由我來處理。」鷹眼説。

P. 84

鷹眼披著熊皮走出洞穴，何歐跟著走在後頭。他發現四周有二十來個心急如焚的親友圍了上來。生病婦女的父親和丈夫對著他們走過來。

「弟兄，魔驅走了嗎？這手裡抱著的是什麼？」父親問。

「是您的女兒。鬼魂已經離開她的身體，被關在洞穴裡了。我現在要帶她到一個地方，讓她的精氣神恢復。」何歐説。

「那你們走

吧，我們會在洞穴外面等，要是鬼魂走出來，我們就用棍棒對付他！」

婦女的父親和丈夫拔出戰斧，守在洞口。其他的婦女和小孩，則是去折樹枝或是撿石頭，做著同樣的準備。何歐和鷹眼很快地鑽進樹林裡。

野外新鮮的空氣，讓愛麗絲甦醒了過來。她人還很虛，不過還能自己走路。

「沿著這條路就能走到河邊。你們走下去，然後爬上右手邊的山丘，那裡有一個達拉威村落，你們去哪裡尋求庇護就安全了。」鷹眼説。

「那你呢？」何歐問。

「安卡斯還在胡龍人的手裡，他是摩希根人最後的血脈，我一定要去救他！」鷹眼説。

加慕正用著校音笛吹曲子時，大熊悄悄地潛進屋子裡來。加慕嚇得出神，大熊抖抖一身的濃毛，發出一聲叫吼，然後説：「加慕，把你的校音笛放下。」

「你是什麼東西？」加慕驚恐地説。

「不就是我嘛。」鷹眼一邊説道，一邊挪開毛茸茸的熊頭。

加慕喃喃地謝天謝地。

「愛麗絲和何歐已經沒事了，現在，我要找到安卡斯。」鷹眼説。

「他被關起來了。」加慕説。

「帶我去找他。」鷹眼説。

P. 86

胡龍人戰士站到一旁讓加慕走進棚屋，他們看到加慕的身旁跟著一個披著熊皮的巫醫。戰士們想跟進去觀看巫醫做法。鷹眼往地上一坐，吼了一聲。

「巫醫怕他做法時會連累到各位弟兄，

把各位給嚇壞了，所以請各位站得遠一點。」加慕說。

胡龍人立刻從棚屋口退回原地。鷹眼和加慕走進棚屋，屋子裡只有一點點火光，安卡斯坐在一個角落裡，手腳都被綑住。一開始，安卡斯以為是敵人送進來一隻熊要對付他，所以閉上眼睛，將身體緊緊挨著牆。未料，大熊竟發出像蛇那樣的嘶嘶聲。安卡斯靠近觀察這隻野獸。

「鷹眼！」安卡斯叫道。

「快把他鬆開！」鷹眼對加慕說。

鷹眼脫下熊皮，拿出一把閃閃發亮的長刀，交給安卡斯。

「外面有胡龍人，我再把熊皮披上，做調虎離山之計。」

安卡斯把雙臂交叉抱在胸前，身體仰靠在牆上。

「安卡斯不走，他要和父親的兄弟並肩戰鬥，和摩希根人的朋友同生死。」安卡斯說。

「我很高興聽到你這樣說。不然這樣好了，熊皮給你披，你一定可以演好熊這個角色的。」鷹眼說。

P. 87

鷹眼轉向加慕，說道：「你拿我的獵衫和帽子，我拿你的毯子和帽子。你的書本、眼鏡和校音笛也都給我，如果可以的話。等我們之後碰面，我會全數歸還。你要是決定留下，那你就坐在暗處，假裝成安卡斯。你可以衝出去，也可以留在這裡。」

「我留在這裡。」加慕說。

鷹眼和加慕握了握手。接著他和披上熊皮的安卡斯走出棚屋，鷹眼則在胡龍人的面前裝成加慕的樣子，模仿加慕的動作。鷹眼唱著聖歌，不時配合著歌曲揮舞手臂，學得很像加慕。他們兩個人慢慢地往前走，裝做沒事的樣子。

在他們快走到林子邊時，棚屋裡傳來了很大一聲叫聲。安卡斯站挺身子，搖掉身上的大熊皮。這時身後一片叫喊聲，鷹眼和安卡斯繼續往前走，隨即安全地躲進了林子的陰暗處。

逃脫

• 用你自己的話來描繪以下的逃脫情形：

　□ 愛麗絲和何歐的逃脫

　□ 安卡斯和鷹眼的逃脫

• 你想加慕發生了什麼事？

CHAPTER 15

P. 88

那些印地安人在棚屋外守著。他們不想被巫醫的巫術給害到，但又耐不住性子，很想看棚屋裡是怎麼做法的，就小心翼翼、提心吊膽走到門邊，朝門的縫隙往裡面窺探。他們看到安卡斯坐在火堆旁，便盯著他瞧了片刻。這時，他轉過臉來，他們認出了那是加慕。他們大聲一吼，衝進棚屋，抓住加慕。

加慕心想自己大限已到。印地安人想報復，他手上這時已經沒有聖經和校音笛，但他可以憑記憶唱出一些片段。他為自己唱起安魂曲，準備迎接死後世界的來臨。印地安人看到他這個舉動，想

起他的腦子有毛病，就扔下他離開。

　　沒多久，俘虜逃走的事情傳遍整個村落。兩百多名戰士聚集在棚屋前面，聽候酋長的追捕令。然而，有一個重要的人物卻遲遲沒有出現。

　　「馬瓜在哪裡？」一位酋長問。

　　「去他的屋子找他，快叫他過來，這裡需要他。」另一個酋長說。

　　這些最德高望重的酋長聚在一起商討情況。這時生病婦人的父親來到會場，跟酋長們說了巫醫治病的事，還說有一隻奇怪的大熊尾隨他們進到了洞裡。會議上於是派了十名最有智慧的酋長前去調查。

P. 89

　　在黑暗無聲的洞穴裡，他們發現生病的婦女還躺在自己的床上。

　　「這不可能啊！我們明明看到巫醫抱著她走進樹林裡的啊。」一個酋長說。

　　婦女的父親趕到床邊，彎下身仔細打量女兒的臉。突然，他發出悲慟的哭喊聲：「大神對兒女們生氣了！我女兒死了！」

　　一個酋長正開口說話時，一個聲音打斷了他。隔壁房間裡滾出了一團黑黑的東西，滾到了洞穴中央。

　　「是馬瓜！」戰士喊道。他們看到這位胡龍酋長那張憤怒猙獰的臉。

　　馬瓜從手到腳都被綁住。他們幫他鬆開後，馬瓜站起來，一臉鐵青。

　　「那個摩希根人，一定要讓他死！」馬瓜發出雷聲般的怒吼。

　　房間裡鴉雀無聲。後來有一個酋長說道：「摩希根人跑得很快，但我們的年輕戰士還是抓得到他。」

　　「他逃跑了？你們竟然讓他給逃跑了？」馬瓜問。

　　「這不是我們的錯，是有邪靈在作怪，騙過了我們的眼睛。」酋長說。

　　馬瓜輕蔑地說：「邪靈？這個邪靈奪走了我們那麼多胡龍人的命，取走了我們戰士的頭皮，而且還把我綁起來，扔在這個洞穴裡！」

　　「朋友，你指的是誰？」

　　「我指的是那個有著胡龍人的心眼、像胡龍人一樣狡猾的白人。我說的就是鷹眼！」馬瓜說。

P. 90

　　翌日，天一破曉就來了二十名戰士，等候在馬瓜的屋外。會議上決定由馬瓜負責這次的行動。人馬現在準備就緒，他領著大家悄悄通過一條蜿蜒的小溪，沿著小湖前進。在他們一路走過時，身後的岩石堆裡冒出了一隻大水獺，興味盎然地打量著他們。在戰士們步入樹林後，大水獺從岩石堆中走出來，脫下毛皮面具，露出摩希根人欽加哥那張嚴肅的臉。

P.91

當天稍晚，馬瓜來到了達拉威的村落。

「歡迎聰明的胡龍人到來！」達拉威的一位酋長說。

「我的俘虜沒給你們添麻煩吧？」馬瓜說。

P.92

「我們也很歡迎她。」達拉威酋長說。

「如果她給兄弟帶來困擾，我就把她帶回去。」馬瓜說。

「不，我們歡迎她來。」酋長重複說道。

「我在樹林裡看到一些可疑的足跡，你們村子裡也有發現嗎？」馬瓜看看四周說道。

「兄弟，你指的是誰？」酋長問。

「我指的是我們不共戴天的仇人——鷹眼！長來福！」馬瓜說。

酋長對旁邊的人耳語了幾句話，之後來了更多的戰士和重要的酋長加入討論。他們聽到馬瓜所帶來的消息，無不表示驚訝與擔心。這個達拉威會議決定召開全族大會。

隔天一大早，一千名戰士聚在棚屋外面，等候酋長的命令。有三個人站到眾人前面，這三個人的年紀都很大，其中一個需要人攙扶，他的歲數有上百歲了。這個老者拖著腳步，舉步艱難地緩緩移動。他一張黝黑的雞皮臉，和一頭長長的蒼蒼白髮形成對比。戰士們小聲說出他的名字「撻門納」。撻門納的智慧和公正，眾所周知，而且他有能力和大神溝通。

大批人群繞著這個老者和其他的大會人員，現場一片肅靜。不久，一批戰士押著俘虜走過來。

智慧

• 說一個人具有智慧，是指什麼？

• 寫下你的答案，和別人分享看法。

• 你認為有誰是具有智慧的？

CHAPTER 16

P.93

蔻若站在那裡，用手臂挽住愛麗絲。面對周圍這些表情凶狠的印地安人，她依舊面不改色。站在她旁邊的是何歐，站在她後面的是鷹眼，裡頭沒有看到安卡斯。在撻門納這批老酋長中，有一個人用英語問：「哪一位是長來福？」

沒有人答話。何歐注意到馬瓜的眼睛在凝視著蔻若，而蔻若也鎮靜地看著馬瓜。馬瓜抓住愛麗絲的手臂，準備把她帶走。蔻若跑到撻門納的跟前跪下。

P.95

蔻若大聲說道：「公正高尚的達拉威人，我們仰靠您的智慧和慈悲！您年高德劭，看遍了世間的惡，請不要相信馬瓜這個人！他會用謊言毒害您的耳朵，他是個嗜血的惡魔。」

眾人看著撻門納，靜待他的回應。這位老者站起來，開始說話。

「你是什麼人？」撻門納問。

「我來自你們所痛恨的種族，但我不曾傷害過你們的人，我在這裡向您求助。

請您告訴我，撻門納是一個為人父者嗎？」蔻若說。

老者笑了笑，環顧四周的人群，答道：「是，我是這個部落的父親。」

蔻若繼續說道：「我不為自己請求什麼。那邊的那位年輕女孩，她的父親行將就木，許多人都很疼愛她，而且她很善良，難能可貴，她不應該成為惡人的犧牲品。在那位胡龍人還沒有把她帶走之前，請把我們這邊的一個人叫過來吧。他是你們族裡的人，請聽聽他所說的。」

「他是一個為敵人效命的紅人，我們把他留下，準備拷問他。」一個酋長對撻門納說。

「把他帶上來。」撻門納吩咐說。

不一會兒，安卡斯就被帶到人群的中央。

「這個俘虜是說什麼語言的？」撻門納問。

「他說著跟祖先一樣的語言，達拉威語。」安卡斯回答。

「你是什麼人？」撻門納問道。

P.96

「安卡斯，欽加哥的兒子。」安卡斯站在眾人面前，驕傲地說。

現在在日光下，撻門納看到安卡斯的胸前刺了一隻小小的藍色烏龜圖騰。

「我的族人是部落的祖先，我是偉大的『搗拿密烏龜』的子孫！」安卡斯說。

老者張大眼睛，高喊道：「撻門納的時代要結束了！感謝大神！終於有人可以接任我主持會議了！我們找到了安卡斯，欽加哥的兒子！現在，即將離世的老鷹，可以望向東昇的太陽了！」

CHAPTER 17

P.97

安卡斯驕傲地站在撻門納的旁邊，群眾都可以看到他。

「這是事實，許多酋長的身體都流著烏龜的血，但這些人都已經離開人世，只剩下欽加哥和他的兒子了。」安卡斯說。

安卡斯朝人群裡望去，他看到了雙手被縛住的鷹眼。他立刻走向他的朋友，切斷繩子，把鷹眼帶到撻門納的旁邊。

「父親，這個白人，是一個正人君子，他是達拉威人的朋友。」安卡斯說。

撻門納點了點頭，問道：「那胡龍人帶來我們村子裡的這位女士呢？」

「她是我的人！」馬瓜一邊喊道，一邊對安卡斯搖著勝利的手勢。

安卡斯沒有回應他。

「我的兒子很沉默。」撻門納說。

「摩希根人,你知道她是我的人!」馬瓜說。

「沒有錯,但請不要讓馬瓜帶走她。」安卡斯難過地說。

「馬瓜的家空蕩蕩的,他需要自己的妻子和小孩。」馬瓜說。

撻門納轉向蔻若,問道:「女孩,你願意嗎?一個偉大的戰士想要你當他的妻子。你跟著他,就不會斷了血脈。你們的子孫後代會一直持續下去。」

「我寧可死去,也不願意接受這種屈辱。」蔻若說。

「胡龍人,她的心在自己父母親的篷帳裡。勉強得到的婚姻,不會有幸福的家庭。」撻門納說。

「請撻門納發話吧。」馬瓜說。

P.98

愛情

• 馬瓜想娶蔻若,但是蔻若不願意嫁給他。你覺得在一段良好的關係中,有哪些因素是不可或缺的?請寫下三點。

「這個人是你帶來的,你就把她帶走吧。大神不允許我們做不公正的事。」撻門納說。

馬瓜走向前抓住蔻若的手臂。

「等等!胡龍人,你行行好!這位白人的贖金,可以讓你有享不完的榮華富貴!」何歐說。

「馬瓜是紅人,他才不需要白人的錢!」

馬瓜推著蔻若往前走。

「我不用你趕,我等一下就來。」蔻若說。

愛麗絲昏厥過去,倒在何歐的手臂裡。蔻若彎下身,親吻了一下愛麗絲後,對馬瓜說:「我現在就走。」

她跟著馬瓜一行人從人群中穿過。

「馬瓜,達拉威人不能阻擋你,但是我可以!」何歐說。

「不,不要跟上去,你會沒命的。」鷹眼說。

「胡龍人,你看看太陽,等太陽升上樹梢時,我們就會追上你。」安卡斯說。

「達拉威人,你們這班走狗!兔崽子!死賊!我啐你們一臉!」馬瓜答道。他在帶著蔻若走進樹林之前,又回頭對何歐和安卡斯做了一個輕蔑的表情。

CHAPTER 18

P.100

當太陽高高升到了天際，安卡斯將戰斧對著一棵樹擲過去，發出了很大一聲喊殺聲。年輕的戰士們全副武裝，他們塗上彩紋，準備戰鬥。安卡斯準備帶著他們去搜尋敵人。

何歐把愛麗絲留下，讓達拉威婦女來照顧她，然後加入鷹眼的人馬之中。安卡斯派了二十名戰士給鷹眼，他召集酋長，發號施令。最後，他帶著兩百多名戰士，從村落裡出發。

他們在樹林裡停下來商討策略。這時，遠方突然出現一個身影。

「那一定是馬瓜的戰士。」安卡斯說。

「他的死期到了。」鷹眼說罷，便舉槍瞄準，但又隨即把槍放下。

「我以為是胡龍人，我錯啦！」鷹眼說。

那個緊張兮兮朝著達拉威人走過來的人，是加慕！他一看到安卡斯和鷹眼這些老面孔，立刻流露出喜悅的表情。

「你有遇到胡龍人嗎？」鷹眼問。

「他們躲在林子裡，到處都是他們的人。」加慕說。

「馬瓜呢？」安卡斯問。

P.101

「他也在裡頭，蔻若跟他在一起，他把她關在山洞裡。」加慕說。

「我帶戰士沿著這條溪走過去，去跟欽加哥和穆羅會合，我會再打信號給你。安卡斯，你們從正面過去。只要胡龍人在我們的射程內，我們就開火。之後，我們再去山洞裡把蔻若救出來。」鷹眼說。

他們周詳地討論計畫，一切安排妥當之後，鷹眼就帶著戰士朝溪流前進。鷹眼停住腳步，等所有戰士到齊，他用達拉威語和他們交談。

「各位，我們就在這裡守株待兔，等胡龍人的氣味飄過來。」鷹眼接著轉向加慕，說：「記住，不可以唱歌。我發號施令時，只能響起槍聲。」

加慕點點頭。鷹眼做了個手勢，要大家繼續前進。

然而他們走了沒幾步，就傳來槍聲，一個達拉威戰士應聲倒下。

「注意隱蔽！」鷹眼喊道。

達拉威人戒備地往前推進，他們不斷放槍，何歐也跟著大夥做。胡龍人藏身在樹幹後面，向他們反擊。胡龍人的子彈從四面八方過來，但鷹眼知道這時候「退」比「進」更危險，對方的人馬

似乎正對著他們包圍過來。不過就在這時，傳來了安卡斯和戰士們的喊殺聲。

P.102

「往前衝！」鷹眼大喊道。

達拉威人衝向胡龍人，雙方展開近身攻擊。胡龍人節節敗退，一直退到濃密的樹林邊，然後鑽進樹叢裡藏身。未料胡龍人的身後這時也傳來槍火聲，鷹眼他們聽到了一個凶猛的喊殺聲。

「是欽加哥！胡龍人現在腹背受敵了！」鷹眼說。

胡龍人戰士無處可藏，他們四下逃命，躲開達拉威人的子彈和戰斧。有人逃過一劫，卻有更多的人命喪黃泉。

「小心，會有更多的胡龍人攻過來。」鷹眼說。

何歐看著欽加哥。欽加哥不動聲色地坐在一塊岩石上。

「達拉威人發動攻擊的時候到了！」何歐說。

「還沒，欽加哥在等待時機。」鷹眼回答

這時，欽加哥發出喊殺聲，達拉威人一陣掃射，十幾個胡龍人應聲倒下。林子裡這時又發出另一聲喊殺聲，胡龍人一陣混亂，安卡斯帶著上百名戰士從林子裡殺出來。達拉威人追擊胡龍人，有一小批胡龍人脫隊，他們慢慢爬上山丘，當中可以赫見表情特別高傲且凶狠的馬瓜。

P.104

安卡斯一看見馬瓜，大吼了一聲，六、七個戰士隨即跟上來。看到安卡斯

逼近，馬瓜笑了笑，因為他的人馬比安卡斯多。馬瓜舉槍瞄準，然而就在他準備開槍之際，鷹眼帶人趕了過來。馬瓜立刻掉頭，爬上山丘撤退。

安卡斯、鷹眼和穆羅，他們和馬瓜這邊的胡龍人一番激戰後，地上躺滿了屍首。有兩名戰士跟著馬瓜逃脫，避開了混戰。安卡斯跑上山丘，尋找馬瓜的蹤影，鷹眼、何歐和加慕跟隨在後。馬瓜鑽進濃密的樹叢，然後走進了一個山洞裡。

「我們找到他了！」鷹眼喊道。

他們一行人跟著走進山洞，胡龍人已經消失在長長的甬道裡。這時，他們看到有人穿著一件白色的衣服。

「是蔻若！」何歐喊道。

有兩個胡龍人正拖著蔻若走，走在他們前面的是馬瓜。

「站住！胡龍狗！」安卡斯揮舞戰斧，對馬瓜大聲喝道。

蔻若在岩崖邊停下腳步，腳下是一道很深的瀑布。

「我不走了！胡龍人，要殺要剮，隨你。我不走了！」蔻若喊道。

「女人家！你是要住馬瓜的房子，還是要挨馬瓜的刀子？你自己選！」馬瓜說。

P.105

馬瓜舉起手，手上的刀子在光線下閃閃發光。他躊躇了一下，又把手放下。他看著蔻若，露出為難的表情。就在這時，他們上方傳來一聲吼叫，只見安卡斯跳下來出現在他們眼前。馬瓜吃驚地往後退了一步。

這時，馬瓜的一個戰士抓住蔻若，把

刀子刺進蔻若的胸腔裡，蔻若隨即倒地而亡。馬瓜一看，非常憤怒和震驚，他想攻擊戰士，但他們中間隔著安卡斯。馬瓜舉起刀子，發出一聲大吼，往安卡斯的背部戳進去。安卡斯站起來，把殺害蔻若的凶手打倒在腳下。

安卡斯轉過身，看著馬瓜。馬瓜揪住安卡斯的手，對準這個摩希根人的胸膛，一連捅上好幾刀。安卡斯用蔑視的神情，盯著馬瓜。最後，他從馬瓜的手中滑下，倒在馬瓜的腳邊，斷氣身亡。

戰鬥

- 在爭奪蔻若的打鬥過程中，發生了哪些事情？
- 和夥伴討論，寫下一步步所發生的事情。
- 想想以下這些人在打鬥的過程中，發生了什麼事？
  ☐ 蔻若　☐ 鷹眼　☐ 何歐
  ☐ 馬瓜　☐ 安卡斯

P.106

何歐在岩壁上目睹這一幕，驚駭不已。

「你發發慈悲！」何歐喊道。

馬瓜對著何歐揮動血淋淋的刀子，發出勝利的吼叫聲。這個聲音傳到了千尺之下的山谷裡，正在那裡打鬥的每一個人都聽到了聲音。鷹眼沿著懸崖奔過來，但看到的只剩下屍體。

「抓住他！」鷹眼大喊。

馬瓜跳過岩石溝，鷹眼和加慕沒逮著。

「他要是跳到那邊的懸崖上，我們就追不到了。」加慕說。

馬瓜站在峻峭的懸崖邊，他只要往前一躍，再差一步就安全無虞了。他停下

來，對鷹眼晃著空拳。

「白人是狗！達拉威人是孬種！馬瓜把他們留在岩石上餵烏鴉啦！」馬瓜喊道。

他哈哈大笑，接著縱身一跳。然而，他沒有算準距離，跳得不夠遠。他伸手死命抓住一株灌木，開始往上爬。

鷹眼舉起槍瞄準，發射！馬瓜的手臂一鬆，身體軟了下來。他轉過頭盯著鷹眼，帶著抵死不屈的憤怒表情。他鬆開手中的灌木，頭部朝下地掉落山崖，最後掉進了山谷裡。

CHAPTER 19

P.107

第二天，達拉威部落沉浸在一片悲傷的哀悼之中。英國和法國的軍官都來參加了葬禮。有六個黑髮的達拉威女孩，她們將香草和樹林裡摘來的野花，灑在蔻若的屍體上。穆羅就坐在蔻若的腳邊，他老淚縱橫，一旁站低低垂著頭的加慕。

族人把安卡斯的遺體放置在王位上。安卡斯坐在那裡，穿著華麗的袍子，戴著閃閃發光的飾品，頭上插著一根鮮艷的羽毛。欽加哥坐在兒子的面前，一動也不動，凝視著兒子的臉。鷹眼站在欽加哥的旁邊，身體倚著他的來福槍。撻門納由兩個酋長攙扶著觀禮，他神情哀傷地望著群眾。

「你為什麼要拋下我們？你的光芒勝過日中的太陽。年輕的戰士，你走了，在你回去靈界的路上，有上百個達拉威人在為你開闢道路。」一位戰士對著死去的

安卡斯説。

達拉威婦女抬著蔻若的遺體，前往下葬的地點。加慕對著填墓，讀誦聖經。

「蔻若，我的孩子，你的父親非常悲痛，他為你獻上禱詞。」穆羅看看何歐和加慕，又説：「紳士們，來吧，我們在這裡的任務已經結束，我們走吧！」

還在啜泣不已的愛麗絲，爬上人們為她準備的馬車。他們向鷹眼揮揮手，坐上馬背，策馬進入樹林，後面跟著一行軍官。

P.108

鷹眼走回欽加哥的身邊，印地安人正在為安卡斯下葬。安卡斯的遺體面對著太陽升起的方向，身旁放著打仗和打獵用的武器和工具，為他最後的旅行做好準備。達拉威人把墓穴掩蓋好，以防動物侵擾。

「我的兄弟們何以悲傷？我的女兒們何以哭泣？一個年輕人已經去了獵場樂園，一個酋長光榮地結束了他的一生。他很有本事，而且英勇過人，善盡職責，大神就需要這樣的戰士，所以召喚了安卡斯。」欽加哥説。

欽加哥看看四周，又説：「我的族人離開了鹽湖湖畔，離開了達拉威的山岳，如今只剩下我孤身一人。」

「不！不！我們的膚色雖然不同，但上帝讓我們走上同一條道路。你不是孤身一人！」鷹眼喊道。

欽加哥溫暖地握住鷹眼的手，他們一起低下頭，眼淚撲漱漱地掉落在地上，

像雨滴一樣滋潤著安卡斯的墳墓。

「我已經活夠了，我的日子太長了。在我的黑夜尚未到來之前，我活著看到了有智慧的摩希根族的最後一位戰士。」撻門納開口説道。

ANSWER KEY

Before Reading

Page 9

4

1. c 2. g 3. f 4. a 5. h
6. e 7. d 8. b

5

1. canoe 2. hoofs 3. moccasins
4. tomahawk 5. knife 6. wigwam
7. cave 8. rifle

Page 10

7 a. 3 b. 6 c. 5 d. 2 e. 1 f. 4

8 1. F 2. T 3. T

Page 25

• Alice doesn't trust Magua because he frightened her when he ran past her horse and she doesn't feel safe with him.
• Hawkeye doesn't trust Magua because he is a Huron and Hurons are thieves.

Page 35

• Cora sends Hawkeye and the Mohicans away because she doesn't want them to die. She asks them to go to her father and get help for her, Alice and Heyward.

Page 49

• A French soldier is coming towards them.
• Hawkeye tells them to get their weapons ready so they will be able to defend themselves in case they are attacked.

Page 59

• Montcalm means that it easier to understand a foreign language than to speak it well.

Page 67

They know Cora is still alive because:
a) they find a piece of her veil;
b) they find her tracks;
c) they find Gamut's whistle.

Page 105

• One of Magua's warriors stabs Cora in the heart.
• Hawkeye follows Magua into a cave and along rocks.
• Heyward watches in horror as Magua stabs Uncas.
• Magua tries to escape with Cora. He kills Uncas and tries to escape by jumping over a precipice, but falls to his death.
• Magua stabs Uncas and kills him.

After Reading

Page 112   A Questions

• Colonel Munro was the commander of Fort William Henry.
• Montcalm was French.
• Magua belonged to the Huron tribe.
• Heyward and his party got lost because Magua brought them the wrong way.
• Cora and Alice went by horse, and the others on foot.
• Gamut was injured.

Page 112   B Questions

• They spoke the language of the Indians.
• Chingachgook means Big Snake.
• Hawkeye was 'The Long Rifle'.
• Cora's mother was from the West Indies.
• Magua wants to take Cora as his wife.

- Uncas and Cora are killed at the end of the story.

Page 113

9

a. 3 b. 1 c. 5 d. 2 e. 4

10

a. 1 b. 11 c. 5 d. 4 e. 8 f. 12
g. 6 h. 7 i. 9 j. 3 k. 10 l. 2

Page 114

12 Alice: a, b, d, f Cora: c, e, g

Page 115

14

a. Uncas b. Gamut c. Heyward
d. Chingachgook e. Colonel Munro
f. Hawkeye g. Magua
h. General Webb i. Montcalm

16 (Possible Answers)

- a. They are friends
- b. They are sisters
- c. They are attracted to each other. Half-way through the book Heyward asks Colonel Munro for Alice's hand in marriage.
- d. Magua want Cora as his wife but Cora despises him.
- e. Munro and Montcalm are enemies but they reach an agreement for the surrender of Fort William Henry.

Page 116

(Possibile Answers)

17 a *and/or* d

19 a, b, d, e

Page 117

22 a. 1 b. 4 c. 3 d. 2

Test

Page 118

1 a. 6 b. 1 c. 5 d. 3 e. 2 f. 4

2 (Possible Answers)

- a. Has Gamut ever used a compass?
- b. Have Alice and Cora ever ridden a horse?
- c. Has Heyward ever learned a foreign language?
- d. Has Cora ever been married?
- e. Has Chingachgook ever visited the graves of his fathers?
- f. Have Magua and Montcalm ever met?

Page 119

3

- a. Has Gamut ever used a compass? →I don't know. I think he has/hasn't.
- b. Have Alice and Cora ever ridden a horse? →Yes, they have.
- c. Has Heyward ever learned a foreign language?→Yes, he has.
- d. Has Cora ever been married?→No, she hasn't.
- e. Has Chingachgook ever visited the graves of his fathers?→No, he hasn't.
- f. Have Magua and Montcalm ever met?→Yes, they have.

4

a. How long
b. How many
c. How long
d. How many
e. How old
f. How long
g. How old

5

a. was able to/managed to
b. wasn't able to
c. was able to
d. wasn't able to
e. didn't manage to
f. wasn't able to

國家圖書館出版品預行編目資料

大地英豪：最後一個摩希根人 / James Fenimore
Cooper 著；安卡斯 譯 . 一初版 . 一 [臺北市]：寂
天文化，2012.3 面；公分 .

中英對照

ISBN 978-986-184-975-1 (25K 平裝附光碟片)

1. 英語   2. 讀本

805.18   101002385

■作者 _ James Fenimore Cooper ■改寫 _ Janet Olearski ■譯者 _ 安卡斯
■主編 _ 黃鈺云 ■製程管理 _ 黃敏昭 ■文字校對 _ 陳慧莉
■出版者 _ 寂天文化事業股份有限公司 ■電話 _ 02-2365-9739 ■傳真 _ 02-2365-9835
■網址 _ www.icosmos.com.tw ■讀者服務 _ onlineservice@icosmos.com.tw
■出版日期 _ 2012年3月 初版一刷（250101）
■郵撥帳號 _ 1998620-0 寂天文化事業股份有限公司
■訂購金額600 （含）元以上郵資免費 ■訂購金額600元以下者，請外加郵資60元
■若有破損，請寄回更換 ■版權所有，請勿翻印